T0110655

Rex Stout

REX STOUT, the creator of Nero Wolfe, was born in Noblesville, Indiana, in 1886, the sixth of nine children of John and Lucetta Todhunter Stout, both Quakers. Shortly after his birth, the family moved to Wakarusa, Kansas. He was educated in a country school, but, by the age of nine, he was recognized throughout the state as a prodigy in arithmetic. Mr. Stout briefly attended the University of Kansas, but left to enlist in the Navy and spent the next two years as a warrant officer on board President Theodore Roosevelt's yacht. When he left the Navy in 1908, Rex Stout began to write free-lance articles, worked as a sightseeing guide and as an itinerant bookkeeper. Later he devised and implemented a school banking system which was installed in four hundred cities and towns throughout the country. In 1927 Mr. Stout retired from the world of finance and, with the proceeds of his banking scheme, left for Paris to write serious fiction. He wrote three novels that received favorable reviews before turning to detective fiction. His first Nero Wolfe novel, *Fer-de-Lance*, appeared in 1934. It was followed by many others, among them, *Too Many Cooks*, *The Silent Speaker*, *If Death Ever Slept*, *The Doorbell Rang*, and *Please Pass the Guilt*, which established Nero Wolfe as a leading character on a par with Erle Stanley Gardner's famous protagonist, Perry Mason. During World War II, Rex Stout waged a personal campaign against Nazism as chairman of the War Writers' Board, master of ceremonies of the radio program "Speaking of Liberty," and as a member of several national committees. After the war, he turned his attention to mobilizing public opinion against the wartime use of thermonuclear devices, was an active leader in the Authors' Guild and resumed writing his Nero Wolfe novels. Rex Stout died in 1975 at the age of eighty-nine. A month before his death, he published his seventy-second Nero Wolfe mystery, *A Family Affair*. Ten years later, a seventy-third Nero Wolfe mystery was discovered and published in *Death Times Three*.

The Rex Stout Library

REX STOUT

Curtains for Three

Introduction
by Judith Kelman

BANTAM BOOKS
NEW YORK • TORONTO • LONDON • SYDNEY • AUCKLAND

A NERO WOLFE MYSTERY

CURTAINS FOR THREE

A Bantam Crime Line Book / published by arrangement
with Viking Penguin, Inc.

PUBLISHING HISTORY

Viking edition published December 1950
Bantam edition / June 1955
Bantam reissue edition / December 1994

Acknowledgment is made to THE AMERICAN MAGAZINE in which these three short
novels originally appeared: *Bullet for One*, July 1948; *The Gun with Wings*,
December 1949; and *Disguise for Murder*, under the title *The Twisted Scarf*,
September 1950.

CRIME LINE and the portrayal of a boxed "cl" are trademarks of Bantam
Books, a division of Bantam Doubleday Dell Publishing Group, Inc.

All rights reserved.
Copyright © 1948, 1949, 1950 by Rex Stout.
Introduction copyright © 1994 by Judith Kelman.
Cover art copyright © 1994 by Tom Hallman.
No part of this book may be reproduced or transmitted in any form or by
any means, electronic or mechanical, including photocopying, recording, or
by any information storage and retrieval system, without permission in
writing from the publisher.
For information address: Viking Press, Penguin USA, 375 Hudson Street,
New York, NY 10014.

ISBN: 978-0-553-76294-5

Bantam Books are published by Bantam Books, a division of Bantam Doubleday Dell Publishing Group, Inc. Its trademark, consisting of the words "Bantam
Books" and the portrayal of a rooster, is Registered in U.S. Patent and Trademark Office and in other countries. Marca Registrada. Bantam Books, 1540
Broadway, New York, New York 10036.

Introduction

Mysteries are a mind game. Lovers of the form are drawn to the puzzle. Who done it and why? Will good triumph over evil and how? In the pulse-pounding race to the solution, will the writer or the reader cross the finish line first?

In this particular sport, the most important muscles are the theoretical ones between the participants' ears. Intellect is everything. A canny detective armed with gobs of gray matter will beat out the Uzi-wielding bad guy every time.

Which partly explains the enduring appeal of Nero Wolfe.

Wolfe is the large lump of calm at the center of the storm's eye in Rex Stout's eponymous mystery series. Evil doesn't move Nero Wolfe. Nothing, short of a good meal or a serious beer shortage, could. This supersleuth is a supersloth, so unfit and lazy he lacks the steam to lean over and retrieve a weighty retainer check from his desk.

For that and other onerous physical chores, he has Archie Goodwin, his fleet-footed, lighthearted, adventurous assistant. While Archie does all necessary legwork and Fritz, Wolfe's household retainer, attends to the master's ravenous appetites, Wolfe's sole responsibility is to sit back and revel in the whirring of his keen, insightful mind.

At the critical moment, the cylinders are guaranteed to click into perfect alignment, allowing Wolfe to finger the suspect from the comfort of his favorite chair in his office in his elegant brownstone on West Thirty-fifth Street.

Of course, the moment must conform to the detective's unyielding schedule. During set mealtimes and the four hours each day Wolfe spends tending his ten thousand orchids, murder and mayhem simply have to wait.

And they do.

In this respect Nero Wolfe is sort of a porky two-legged Club Med: an antidote for the strident intrusiveness and chaos of civilization.

Reality for most of us is ringing phones, boisterous kids, mountains of bills, and demanding bosses. Most of our existences are liberally sprinkled with dark dreams and rude awakenings. Our paths are marred by potholes and sudden detours. Even when things feel settled, we face constant reminders that cataclysmic change can occur at any moment. Much of today's news is a litany of tragic accidents, natural disasters, and unthinkable violence. Life, I tell my sons, is what happens when you're busy making other plans.

That uncertainty invades most contemporary novels of mystery and suspense, often driving the narrative (sometimes off the road). Evil explodes on the fictional scene with all the subtlety of Howard Stern or Madonna. The hapless protagonist is derailed like a sabotaged train. Amateur sleuths spring into frantic action. Law-enforcement professionals haul out their full bags of high- and low-tech forensic tricks and pursue the bad guys like a stampede of crazed buffalo.

Pyrotechnics can dazzle. Car chases and literal cliff-hangers do raise the blood pressure and squeeze out the gasps. But the reader manipulated by such shameless Hollywood devices is being distracted from the heart and soul of the mystery form: the puzzle.

Wolfe's world, on the other hand, is refined, prescribed, predictable. Even when crime presses its noisome finger at his doorbell, Nero Wolfe remains in perfect, unflinching control.

Rex Stout recognized that the smallest detail can speak volumes. He relied solely on intricate plot twists and dazzlingly quiet feats of detection. He had no need or desire to distract his readers from the story's central strand.

Nowhere is this more evident than in *Curtains for Three*, a trio of novelettes first published in 1950. Unsolved crimes are delivered handily to the detective's door. Witnesses and likely perpetrators present themselves and compliantly await Wolfe's audience. In one case the murder conveniently occurs in his office.

If you think that sounds dull, think again. The seventy-three Nero Wolfe mysteries have intrigued and entertained millions of readers and inspired countless writers to tackle the form. Rex Stout has become a virtual synonym for the term *classic mystery*. Mention West Thirty-fifth Street to a mystery fan and the response is sure to be a look of instant recognition and a smile.

If Rex Stout and his stout detective have become a reading addiction, you have plenty of company. If this is your first experience in puzzle solving with the great Nero Wolfe, prepare to settle in and savor. You have plenty of tasty treats yet to enjoy.

—Judith Kelman

Contents

Curtains for Three

The Gun
with Wings

I

The young woman took a pink piece of paper from her handbag, got up from the red leather chair, put the paper on Nero Wolfe's desk, and sat down again. Feeling it my duty to keep myself informed and also to save Wolfe the exertion of leaning forward and reaching so far, I arose and crossed to hand the paper to him after a glance at it. It was a check for five thousand dollars, dated that day, August fourteenth, made out to him, and signed Margaret Mion. He gave a look and dropped it back on the desk.

"I thought," she said, "perhaps that would be the best way to start the conversation."

In my chair at my desk, taking her in, I was readjusting my attitude. When early that Sunday afternoon, she had phoned for an appointment, I had dug up a vague recollection of a picture of her in the paper some months back, and had decided it would be no treat to meet her, but now I was hedging. Her appeal wasn't what she had, which was only so-so, but what she did with it. I don't mean tricks. Her mouth wasn't attractive even when she smiled, but the smile was.

Her eyes were just a pair of brown eyes, nothing at all sensational, but it was a pleasure to watch them move around, from Wolfe to me to the man who had come with her, seated off to her left. I guessed she had maybe three years to go to reach thirty.

"Don't you think," the man asked her, "we should get some questions answered first?"

His tone was strained and a little harsh, and his face matched it. He was worried and didn't care who knew it. With his deep-set gray eyes and well-fitted jaw he might on a happier day have passed for a leader of men, but not as he now sat. Something was eating him. When Mrs. Mion had introduced him as Mr. Frederick Weppler I had recognized the name of the music critic of the *Gazette*, but I couldn't remember whether he had been mentioned in the newspaper accounts of the event that had caused the publication of Mrs. Mion's picture.

She shook her head at him, not arbitrarily. "It wouldn't help, Fred, really. We'll just have to tell it and see what he says." She smiled at Wolfe—or maybe it wasn't actually a smile, but just her way of handling her lips. "Mr. Weppler wasn't quite sure we should come to see you, and I had to persuade him. Men are more cautious than women, aren't they?"

"Yes," Wolfe agreed, and added, "Thank heaven."

She nodded. "I suppose so." She gestured. "I brought that check with me to show that we really mean it. We're in trouble and we want you to get us out. We want to get married and we can't. That is—if I should just speak for myself—I want to marry him." She looked at Weppler, and this time it was unquestionably a smile. "Do you want to marry me, Fred?"

"Yes," he muttered. Then he suddenly jerked his chin up and looked defiantly at Wolfe. "You understand this is embarrassing, don't you? It's none of your business, but we've come to get your help. I'm thirty-four years old, and this is the first time I've ever been—" He stopped. In a moment he said stiffly, "I am in love with Mrs. Mion and I want to marry her more than I have ever wanted anything in my life." His eyes went to his love and he murmured a plea. "Peggy!"

Wolfe grunted. "I accept that as proven. You both want to get married. Why don't you?"

"Because we can't," Peggy said. "We simply can't. It's on account—you may remember reading about my husband's death in April, four months ago? Alberto Mion, the opera singer?"

"Vaguely. You'd better refresh my memory."

"Well, he died—he killed himself." There was no sign of a smile now. "Fred—Mr. Weppler and I found him. It was seven o'clock, a Tuesday evening in April, at our apartment on East End Avenue. Just that afternoon Fred and I had found out that we loved each other, and—"

"Peggy!" Weppler called sharply.

Her eyes darted to him and back to Wolfe. "Perhaps I should ask you, Mr. Wolfe. He thinks we should tell you just enough so you understand the problem, and I think you can't understand it unless we tell you everything. What do you think?"

"I can't say until I hear it. Go ahead. If I have questions, we'll see."

She nodded. "I imagine you'll have plenty of questions. Have you ever been in love but would have died rather than let anyone see it?"

"Never," Wolfe said emphatically. I kept my face straight.

"Well, I was, and I admit it. But no one knew it, not even him. Did you, Fred?"

"I did not." Weppler was emphatic too.

"Until that afternoon," Peggy told Wolfe. "He was at the apartment for lunch, and it happened right after lunch. The others had left, and all of a sudden we were looking at each other, and then he spoke or I did, I don't know which." She looked at Weppler imploringly. "I know you think this is embarrassing, Fred, but if he doesn't know what it was like he won't understand why you went upstairs to see Alberto."

"Does he have to?" Weppler demanded.

"Of course he does." She returned to Wolfe. "I suppose I can't make you see what it was like. We were completely—well, we were in love, that's all, and I guess we had been for quite a while without saying it, and that made it all the more—more overwhelming. Fred wanted to see my husband right away, to tell him about it and decide what we could do, and I said all right, so he went upstairs—"

"Upstairs?"

"Yes, it's a duplex, and upstairs was my husband's soundproofed studio, where he practiced. So he went—"

"Please, Peggy," Weppler interrupted her. His eyes went to Wolfe. "You should have it firsthand. I went up to tell Mion that I loved his wife, and she loved me and not him, and to ask him to be civilized about it. Getting a divorce has come to be regarded as fairly civilized, but he didn't see it that way. He was anything but civilized. He wasn't violent, but he was damned mean. After some of that I got afraid I might do to him what Gif James had done, and I left. I didn't want to go back to Mrs. Mion while I was in that state of mind, so I left the studio by the door to the upper hall and took the elevator there."

He stopped.

"And?" Wolfe prodded him.

"I walked it off. I walked across to the park, and after a while I had calmed down and I phoned Mrs. Mion, and she met me in the park. I told her what Mion's attitude was, and I asked her to leave him and come with me. She wouldn't do that." Weppler paused, and then went on, "There are two complications you ought to have if you're to have everything."

"If they're relevant, yes."

"They're relevant all right. First, Mrs. Mion had and has money of her own. That was an added attraction for Mion. It wasn't for me. I'm just telling you."

"Thank you. And the second?"

"The second was Mrs. Mion's reason for not leaving Mion immediately. I suppose you know he had been the top tenor at the Met for five or six years, and his voice was gone—temporarily. Gifford James, the baritone, had hit him on the neck with his fist and hurt his larynx—that was early in March—and Mion couldn't finish the season. It had been operated, but his voice hadn't come back, and naturally he was glum, and Mrs. Mion wouldn't leave him under those circumstances. I tried to persuade her to, but she wouldn't. I wasn't anything like normal that day, on account of what had happened to me for the first time in my life, and on account of what Mion had said to me, so I wasn't reasonable and I left her in the park and went downtown to a bar and started drinking. A lot of time went by and I had quite a few, but I wasn't pickled. Along toward seven o'clock I decided I had to see her again and carry her off so she wouldn't spend another night there. That mood took me back to East End Avenue and up to the twelfth floor, and then I stood there in the hall a while, perhaps ten minutes, before my finger went to the pushbutton. Finally I rang, and the maid let me in and went for Mrs. Mion, but I had lost my nerve or something. All I did was suggest that we should have a talk with Mion together. She agreed, and we went upstairs and—"

"Using the elevator?"

"No, the stairs inside the apartment. We entered the studio. Mion was on the floor. We went over to him. There was a big hole through the top of his head. He was dead. I led Mrs. Mion out, made her come, and on the stairs—they're too narrow to go two abreast—she fell and rolled halfway down. I carried her to her room and put her on her bed, and I started for the living room, for the phone there, when I thought of something to do first. I went out and took the elevator to the ground floor, got the doorman and elevator man together, and asked them who had been taken up to the Mion apartment, either the twelfth floor or the thirteenth, that afternoon. I said they must be damn sure not to skip anybody. They gave me the names and I wrote them down. Then I went back up to the apartment and phoned the police. After I did that it struck me that a layman isn't supposed to decide if a man is dead, so I phoned Dr. Lloyd, who has an apartment there in the building. He came at once, and I took him up to the studio. We hadn't been there more than three or four minutes when the first policeman came, and of course—"

"If you please," Wolfe put in crossly. "Everything is sometimes too much. You haven't even hinted at the trouble you're in."

"I'll get to it—"

"But faster, I hope, if I help. My memory has been jogged. The doctor and the police pronounced him dead. The muzzle of the revolver had been thrust into his mouth, and the emerging bullet had torn out a piece of his skull. The revolver, found lying on the floor beside him, belonged to him and was kept there in the studio. There was no sign of any struggle and no mark of any other injury on him. The loss of his voice was an excellent motive for suicide. Therefore, after a routine investigation, giving due weight to the difficulty of sticking the barrel of a loaded revolver into a man's mouth without arousing him to protest, it was recorded as suicide. Isn't that correct?"

They both said yes.

"Have the police reopened it? Or is gossip at work?"

They both said no.

"Then let's get on. Where's the trouble?"

"It's us," Peggy said.

"Why? What's wrong with you?"

"Everything." She gestured. "No. I don't mean that—not everything, just one thing. After my husband's death and the—the routine investigation, I went away for a while. When I came back—for the past two months Fred and I have been together some, but it wasn't right—I mean we didn't feel right. Day before yesterday, Friday, I went to friends in Connecticut for the weekend, and he was there. Neither of us knew the other was coming. We talked it out yesterday and last night and this morning, and we decided to come and ask you to help us—anyway, I did, and he wouldn't let me come alone."

Peggy leaned forward and was in deadly earnest. "You *must* help us, Mr. Wolfe. I love him so much—so much!—and he says he loves me, and I know he does! Yesterday afternoon we decided we would get married in October, and then last night we got started talking—but it isn't what we say, it's what is in our eyes when

we look at each other. We just can't get married with
that back of our eyes and trying to hide it—"

A little shiver went over her. "For years—forever?
We can't! We know we can't—it would be horrible!
What it is, it's a question: who killed Alberto? Did he?
Did I? I don't really think he did, and he doesn't really
think I did—I hope he doesn't—but it's there back of
our eyes, and we know it is!"

She extended both hands. "We want you to find
out!"

Wolfe snorted. "Nonsense. You need a spanking or
a psychiatrist. The police may have shortcomings, but
they're not nincompoops. If they're satisfied—"

"But that's it! They wouldn't be satisfied if we had
told the truth!"

"Oh." Wolfe's brows went up. "You lied to them?"

"Yes. Or if we didn't lie, anyhow we didn't tell them
the truth. We didn't tell them that when we first went
in together and saw him, there was no gun lying there.
There was no gun in sight."

"Indeed. How sure are you?"

"Absolutely positive. I never saw anything clearer
than I saw that—that sight—all of it. There was no
gun."

Wolfe snapped at Weppler, "You agree, sir?"

"Yes. She's right."

Wolfe sighed. "Well," he conceded, "I can see that
you're really in trouble. Spanking wouldn't help."

I shifted in my chair on account of a tingle at the
lower part of my spine. Nero Wolfe's old brownstone
house on West Thirty-fifth Street was an interesting
place to live and work—for Fritz Brenner, the chef and
housekeeper, for Theodore Horstmann, who fed and
nursed the ten thousand orchids in the plant rooms up
on the roof, and for me, Archie Goodwin, whose main

field of operations was the big office on the ground floor. Naturally I thought my job the most interesting, since a confidential assistant to a famous private detective is constantly getting an earful of all kinds of troubles and problems—everything from a missing necklace to a new blackmail gimmick. Very few clients actually bored me. But only one kind of case gave me that tingle in the spine: murder. And if this pair of lovebirds were talking straight, this was it.

I I

I had filled two notebooks when they left, more than two hours later.

If they had thought it through before they phoned for an appointment with Wolfe, they wouldn't have phoned. All they wanted, as Wolfe pointed out, was the moon. They wanted him, first, to investigate a four-month-old murder without letting on there had been one; second, to prove that neither of them had killed Alberto Mion, which could be done only by finding out who had; and third, in case he concluded that one of them had done it, to file it away and forget it. Not that they put it that way, since their story was that they were both absolutely innocent, but that was what it amounted to.

Wolfe made it good and plain. "If I take the job," he told them, "and find evidence to convict someone of murder, no matter who, the use I make of it will be solely in my discretion. I am neither an Astraea nor a sadist, but I like my door open. But if you want to drop it now, here's your check, and Mr. Goodwin's notebooks will be destroyed. We can forget you have been here, and shall."

That was one of the moments when they were
within an ace of getting up and going, especially Fred
Weppler, but they didn't. They looked at each other,
and it was all in their eyes. By that time I had about
decided I liked them both pretty well and was even
beginning to admire them, they were so damn determined to get loose from the trap they were in. When
they looked at each other like that their eyes said,
"Let's go and be together, my darling love, and forget
this—come on, come on." Then they said, "It will be so
wonderful!" Then they said, "Yes, oh yes, but— But
we don't want it wonderful for a day or a week; it must
be always wonderful—and we know . . ."

It took strong muscles to hold onto it like that, not
to mention horse sense, and several times I caught
myself feeling sentimental about it. Then of course
there was the check for five grand on Wolfe's desk.

The notebooks were full of assorted matters. There
were a thousand details which might or might not turn
out to be pertinent, such as the mutual dislike between
Peggy Mion and Rupert Grove, her husband's manager, or the occasion of Gifford James socking Alberto
Mion in front of witnesses, or the attitudes of various
persons toward Mion's demand for damages; but you
couldn't use it all, and Wolfe himself never needed
more than a fraction of it, so I'll pick and choose. Of
course the gun was Exhibit A. It was a new one, having been bought by Mion the day after Gifford James
had plugged him and hurt his larynx—not, he had announced, for vengeance on James but for future pro-
tection. He had carried it in a pocket whenever he
went out, and at home had kept it in the studio, lying
on the base of a bust of Caruso. So far as known, it had
never fired but one bullet, the one that killed Mion.

When Dr. Lloyd had arrived and Weppler had

taken him to the studio the gun was lying on the floor not far from Mion's knee. Dr. Lloyd's hand had started for it but had been withdrawn without touching it, so it had been there when the law came. Peggy was positive it had not been there when she and Fred had entered, and he agreed. The cops had made no announcement about fingerprints, which wasn't surprising since none are hardly ever found on a gun that are any good. Throughout the two hours and a half, Wolfe kept darting back to the gun, but it simply didn't have wings.

The picture of the day and the day's people was all filled in. The morning seemed irrelevant, so it started at lunch time with five of them there: Mion, Peggy, Fred, one Adele Bosley, and Dr. Lloyd. It was more professional than social. Fred had been invited because Mion wanted to sell him the idea of writing a piece for the *Gazette* saying that the rumors that Mion would never be able to sing again were malicious hooey. Adele Bosley, who was in charge of public relations for the Metropolitan Opera, had come to help work on Fred. Dr. Lloyd had been asked so he could assure Weppler that the operation he had performed on Mion's larynx had been successful and it was a good bet that by the time the opera season opened in November the great tenor would be as good as ever. Nothing special had happened except that Fred had agreed to do the piece. Adele Bosley and Lloyd had left, and Mion had gone up to the soundproofed studio, and Fred and Peggy had looked at each other and suddenly discovered the most important fact of life since the Garden of Eden.

An hour or so later there had been another gathering, this time up in the studio, around half-past three, but neither Fred nor Peggy had been present. By then Fred had walked himself calm and phoned Peggy, and she had gone to meet him in the park, so their information on the meeting in the studio was hearsay. Besides Mion and Dr. Lloyd there had been four people: Adele Bosley for operatic public relations; Mr. Rupert Grove, Mion's manager; Mr. Gifford James, the baritone who had socked Mion in the neck six weeks previously; and Judge Henry Arnold, James' lawyer. This affair had been even less social than the lunch, having been arranged to discuss a formal request that Mion had made of Gifford James for the payment of a quarter of a million bucks for the damage to Mion's larynx.

Fred's and Peggy's hearsay had it that the conference had been fairly hot at points, with the temperature boosted right at the beginning by Mion's getting the gun from Caruso's bust and placing it on a table at his elbow. On the details of its course they were pretty sketchy, since they hadn't been there, but anyhow the gun hadn't been fired. Also there was plenty of evidence that Mion was alive and well—except for his larynx—when the party broke up. He had made two phone calls after the conference had ended, one to his barber and one to a wealthy female opera patron; his manager, Rupert Grove, had phoned him a little later; and around five-thirty he had phoned downstairs to the maid to bring him a bottle of vermouth and some ice, which she had done. She had taken the tray into the studio, and he had been upright and intact.

I was careful to get all the names spelled right in my notebook, since it seemed likely the job would be to get one of them tagged for murder, and I was especially careful with the last one that got in: Clara James, Gifford's daughter. There were three spotlights on her. First, the reason for James' assault on Mion had been his knowledge or suspicion—Fred and Peggy weren't sure which—that Mion had stepped over the line with

James' daughter. Second, her name had ended the list, got by Fred from the doorman and elevator man, of people who had called that afternoon. They said she had come about a quarter past six and had got off at the floor the studio was on, the thirteenth, and had summoned the elevator to the twelfth floor a little later, maybe ten minutes, and had left. The third spotlight was directed by Peggy, who had stayed in the park a while after Fred had marched off, and had then returned home, arriving around five o'clock. She had not gone up to the studio and had not seen her husband. Sometime after six, she thought around half-past, she had answered the doorbell herself because the maid had been in the kitchen with the cook. It was Clara James. She was pale and tense, but she was always pale and tense. She had asked for Alberto, and Peggy had said she thought he was up in the studio, and Clara had said no, he wasn't there, and never mind. When Clara went for the elevator button, Peggy had shut the door, not wanting company anyway, and particularly not Clara James.

Some half an hour later Fred showed up, and they ascended to the studio together and found that Alberto was there all right, but no longer upright or intact.

That picture left room for a whole night of questions, but Wolfe concentrated on what he regarded as the essentials. Even so, we went into the third hour and the third notebook. He completely ignored some spots that I thought needed filling in; for instance, had Alberto had a habit of stepping over the line with other men's daughters and/or wives, and if so, names please. From things they said I gathered that Alberto had been broad-minded about other men's women, but apparently Wolfe wasn't interested. Along toward the end he was back on the gun again, and when they had nothing new to offer he scowled and got caustic. When they stayed glued he finally snapped at them, "Which one of you is lying?"

They looked hurt. "That won't get you anywhere," Fred Weppler said bitterly, "or us either."

"It would be silly," Peggy Mion protested, "to come here and give you that check and then lie to you. Wouldn't it?"

"Then you're silly," Wolfe said coldly. He pointed a finger at her. "Look here. All of this might be worked out, none of it is preposterous, except one thing. Who put the gun on the floor beside the body? When you two entered the studio it wasn't there; you both swear to that, and I accept it. You left and started downstairs; you fell, and he carried you to your room. You weren't unconscious. Were you?"

"No." Peggy was meeting his gaze. "I could have walked, but he—he wanted to carry me."

"No doubt. He did so. You stayed in your room. He went to the ground floor to compile a list of those who had made themselves available as murder suspects—showing admirable foresight, by the way—came back up and phoned the police and then the doctor, who arrived without delay since he lived in the building. Not more than fifteen minutes intervened between the moment you and Mr. Weppler left the studio and the moment he and the doctor entered. The door from the studio to the public hall on the thirteenth floor has a lock that is automatic with the closing of the door, and the door was closed and locked. No one could possibly have entered during the fifteen minutes. You say that you had left your bed and gone to the living room, and that no one could have used that route without being seen by you. The maid and cook were in the kitchen, unaware of what was going on. So no one entered the studio and placed the gun on the floor."

"Someone did," Fred said doggedly.

Peggy insisted, "We don't know who had a key."

"You said that before." Wolfe was at them now. "Even if everyone had keys, I don't believe it and neither would anyone else." His eyes came to me. "Archie. Would you?"

"I'd have to see a movie of it," I admitted.

"You see?" he demanded of them. "Mr. Goodwin isn't prejudiced against you—on the contrary. He's ready to fight fire for you; see how he gets behind on his notes for the pleasure of watching you look at each other. But he agrees with me that you're lying. Since no one else could have put the gun on the floor, one of you did. I have to know about it. The circumstances may have made it imperative for you, or you thought they did."

He looked at Fred. "Suppose you opened a drawer of Mrs. Mion's dresser to get smelling salts, and the gun was there, with an odor showing it had been recently fired—put there, you would instantly conjecture, by someone to direct suspicion at her. What would you naturally do? Exactly what you did do: take it upstairs and put it beside the body, without letting her know about it. Or—"

"Rot," Fred said harshly. "Absolute rot."

Wolfe looked at Peggy. "Or suppose it was you who found it there in your bedroom, after he had gone downstairs. Naturally you would have—"

"This is absurd," Peggy said with spirit. "How could it have been in my bedroom unless I put it there? My husband was alive at five-thirty, and I got home before that, and was right there, in the living room and my room, until Fred came at seven o'clock. So unless you assume—"

"Very well," Wolfe conceded. "Not the bedroom. But somewhere. I can't proceed until I get this from one of you. Confound it, the gun didn't fly. I expect plenty of lies from the others, at least one of them, but I want the truth from you."

"You've got it," Fred declared.

"No. I haven't."

"Then it's a stalemate." Fred stood up. "Well, Peggy?"

They looked at each other, and their eyes went through the performance again. When they got to the place in the script where it said, "It must be wonderful always," Fred sat down.

But Wolfe, having no part in the script, horned in. "A stalemate," he said dryly, "ends the game, I believe."

Plainly it was up to me. If Wolfe openly committed himself to no dice nothing would budge him. I arose, got the pretty pink check from his desk, put it on mine, placed a paperweight on it, sat down, and grinned at him.

"Granted that you're dead right," I observed, "which is not what you call apodictical, someday we ought to make up a list of the clients that have sat here and lied to us. There was Mike Walsh, and Calida Frost, and that cafeteria guy, Pratt—oh, dozens. But their money was good, and I didn't get so far behind with my notes that I couldn't catch up. All that for nothing?"

"About those notes," Fred Weppler said firmly. "I want to make something clear."

Wolfe looked at him.

He looked back. "We came here," he said, "to tell

you in confidence about a problem and get you to investigate. Your accusing us of lying makes me wonder
if we ought to go on, but if Mrs. Mion wants to I'm
willing. But I want to make it plain that if you divulge
what we've told you, if you tell the police or anyone
else that we said there was no gun there when we
went in, we'll deny it in spite of your damn notes. We'll
deny it and stick to it!" He looked at his girl. "We've
got to, Peggy! All right?"

"He wouldn't tell the police," Peggy declared, with
fair conviction.

"Maybe not. But if he does, you'll stick with me on
the denial. Won't you?"

"Certainly I will," she promised, as if he had asked
her to help kill a rattlesnake.

Wolfe was taking them in, with his lips tightened.
Obviously, with the check on my desk on its way to the
bank, he had decided to add them to the list of clients
who told lies and go on from there. He forced his eyes
wide open to rest them, let them half close again, and
spoke.

"We'll settle that along with other things before
we're through," he asserted. "You realize, of course,
that I'm assuming your innocence, but I've made a
thousand wrong assumptions before now so they're not
worth much. Has either of you a notion of who killed
Mr. Mion?"

They both said no.

He grunted. "I have."

They opened their eyes at him.

He nodded. "It's only another assumption, but I
like it. It will take work to validate it. To begin with, I
must see the people you have mentioned—all six of
them—and I would prefer not to string it out. Since
you don't want them told that I'm investigating a mur-

der, we must devise a stratagem. Did your husband leave a will, Mrs. Mion?"

She nodded and said yes.

"Are you the heir?"

"Yes, I—" She gestured. "I don't need it and don't want it."

"But it's yours. That will do nicely. An asset of the estate is the expectation of damages to be paid by Mr. James for his assault on Mr. Mion. You may properly claim that asset. The six people I want to see were all concerned in that affair, one way or another. I'll write them immediately, mailing the letter tonight special delivery, telling them that I represent you in the matter and would like them to call at my office tomorrow evening."

"That's impossible!" Peggy cried, shocked. "I couldn't! I wouldn't dream of asking Gif to pay damages—"

Wolfe banged a fist on his desk. "Confound it!" he roared. "Get out of here! Go! Do you think murders are solved by cutting out paper dolls? First you lie to me, and now you refuse to annoy people, including the murderer! Archie, put them out!"

"Good for you," I muttered at him. I was getting fed up too. I glared at the would-be clients. "Try the Salvation Army," I suggested. "They're old hands at helping people in trouble. You can have the notebooks to take along—at cost, six bits. No charge for the contents."

They were looking at each other.

"I guess he has to see them somehow," Fred conceded. "He has to have a reason, and I must admit that's a good one. You don't owe them anything—not one of them."

Peggy gave in.

After a few details had been attended to, the most important of which was getting addresses, they left. The manner of their going, and of our speeding them, was so far from cordial that it might have been thought that instead of being the clients they were the prey. But the check was on my desk. When, after letting them out, I returned to the office, Wolfe was leaning back with his eyes shut, frowning in distaste.

I stretched and yawned. "This ought to be fun," I said encouragingly. "Making it just a grab for damages. If the murderer is among the guests, see how long you can keep it from him. I bet he catches on before the jury comes in with the verdict."

"Shut up," he growled. "Blockheads."

"Oh, have a heart," I protested. "People in love aren't supposed to think, that's why they have to hire trained thinkers. You should be happy and proud they picked you. What's a good big lie or two when you're in love? When I saw—"

"Shut up," he repeated. His eyes came open. "Your notebook. Those letters must go at once."

III

Monday evening's party lasted a full three hours, and murder wasn't mentioned once. Even so, it wasn't exactly jolly. The letters had put it straight that Wolfe, acting for Mrs. Mion, wanted to find out whether an appropriate sum could be collected from Gifford James without resort to lawyers and a court, and what sum would be thought appropriate. So each of them was naturally in a state of mind: Gifford James himself; his daughter Clara; his lawyer, Judge Henry Arnold; Adele Bosley for Public Relations; Dr. Nicholas Lloyd

as the technical expert; and Rupert Grove, who had
been Mion's manager. That made six, which was just
comfortable for our big office. Fred and Peggy had not
been invited.

The James trio arrived together and were so punc-
tual, right on the dot at nine o'clock, that Wolfe and I
hadn't yet finished our after-dinner coffee in the office.
I was so curious to have a look that I went to answer
the door instead of leaving it to Fritz, the chef and
house overseer who helps to make Wolfe's days and
years a joy forever almost as much as I do. The first
thing that impressed me was that the baritone took
the lead crossing the threshold, letting his daughter
and his lawyer tag along behind. Since I have occasionally let Lily Rowan share her pair of opera seats with
me, James' six feet and broad shoulders and cocky
strut were nothing new, but I was surprised that he
looked so young, since he must have been close to fifty.
He handed me his hat as if taking care of his hat on
Monday evening, August 15, was the one and only
thing I had been born for. Unfortunately I let it drop.

Clara made up for it by looking at me. That alone
showed she was unusually observant, since one never
looks at the flunkey who lets one in, but she saw me
drop her father's hat and gave me a glance, and then
prolonged the glance until it practically said, "What
are you, in disguise? See you later." That made me feel
friendly, but with reserve. Not only was she pale and
tense, as Peggy Mion had said, but her blue eyes glis-
tened, and a girl her age shouldn't glisten like that.
Nevertheless, I gave her a grin to show that I appreciated the prolonged glance.

Meanwhile the lawyer, Judge Henry Arnold, had
hung up his own hat. During the day I had of course
made inquiries on all of them, and had learned that he

rated the "Judge" only because he had once been a city magistrate. Even so, that's what they called him, so the sight of him was a let-down. He was a little sawed-off squirt with a bald head so flat on top you could have kept an ashtray on it, and his nose was pushed in. He must have been better arranged inside than out, since he had quite a list of clients among the higher levels on Broadway.

Taking them to the office and introducing them to Wolfe, I undertook to assign them to some of the yellow chairs, but the baritone spied the red leather one and copped it. I was helping Fritz fill their orders for drinks when the buzzer sounded and I went back to the front.

It was Dr. Nicholas Lloyd. He had no hat, so that point wasn't raised, and I decided that the searching look he aimed at me was merely professional and automatic, to see if I was anemic or diabetic or what. With his lined handsome face and worried dark eyes he looked every inch a doctor and even surgeon, fully up to the classy reputation my inquiries had disclosed. When I ushered him to the office his eyes lighted up at sight of the refreshment table, and he was the best customer—bourbon and water with mint—all evening.

The last two came together—at least they were on the stoop together when I opened the door. I would probably have given Adele Bosley the red leather chair if James hadn't already copped it. She shook hands and said she had been wanting to meet Archie Goodwin for years, but that was just public relations and went out the other ear. The point is that from my desk I get most of a party profile or three-quarters, but the one in the red leather chair fullface, and I like a view. Not that Adele Bosley was a pin-up, and she must have been in the fifth or sixth grade when Clara

James was born, but her smooth tanned skin and pretty mouth without too much lipstick and nice brown eyes were good scenery.

Rupert Grove didn't shake hands, which didn't upset me. He may have been a good manager for Alberto Mion's affairs, but not for his own physique. A man can be fat and still have integrity, as for instance Falstaff or Nero Wolfe, but that bird had lost all sense of proportion. His legs were short, and it was all in the middle third of him. If you wanted to be polite and look at his face you had to concentrate. I did so, since I needed to size them all up, and saw nothing worthy of recording but a pair of shrewd shifty black eyes.

When these two were seated and provided with liquid, Wolfe fired the starting gun. He said he was sorry it had been necessary to ask them to exert themselves on a hot evening, but that the question at issue could be answered fairly and equitably only if all concerned had a voice in it. The responding murmurs went all the way from acquiescence to extreme irritation. Judge Arnold said belligerently that there was no question at legal issue because Albert Mion was dead.

"Nonsense," Wolfe said curtly. "If that were true, you, a lawyer, wouldn't have bothered to come. Anyway, the purpose of this meeting is to keep it from becoming a legal issue. Four of you telephoned Mrs. Mion today to ask if I am acting for her, and were told that I am. On her behalf I want to collect the facts. I may as well tell you, without prejudice to her, that she will accept my recommendation. Should I decide that a large sum is due her you may of course contest; but if I form the opinion that she has no claim she will bow to it. Under that responsibility I need all the facts. Therefore—"

"You're not a court," Arnold snapped.

"No, sir, I'm not. If you prefer it in a court you'll get it." Wolfe's eyes moved. "Miss Bosley, would your employers welcome that kind of publicity? Dr. Lloyd, would you rather appear as an expert on the witness-stand or talk it over here? Mr. Grove, how would your client feel about it if he were alive? Mr. James, what do you think? You wouldn't relish the publicity either, would you? Particularly since your daughter's name would appear?"

"Why would her name appear?" James demanded in his trained baritone.

Wolfe turned up a palm. "It would be evidence. It would be established that just before you struck Mr. Mion you said to him, 'You let my daughter alone, you bastard.'"

I put my hand in my pocket. I have a rule, justified by experience, that whenever a killer is among those present, or may be, a gun must be handy. Not regarding the back of the third drawer of my desk, where they are kept, as handy enough, the routine is to transfer one to my pocket before guests gather. That was the pocket I put my hand in, knowing how cocky James was. But he didn't leave his chair. He merely blurted, "That's a lie!"

Wolfe grunted. "Ten people heard you say it. That would indeed be publicity, if you denied it under oath and all ten of them, subpoenaed to testify, contradicted you. I honestly think it would be better to discuss it with me."

"What do you want to know?" Judge Arnold demanded.

"The facts. First, the one already moot. When I lie I like to know it. Mr. Grove, you were present when that famous blow was struck. Have I quoted Mr. James correctly?"

"Yes." Grove's voice was a high tenor, which pleased me.

"You heard him say that?"

"Yes."

"Miss Bosley. Did you?"

She looked uncomfortable. "Wouldn't it be better to—"

"Please. You're not under oath, but I'm merely collecting facts, and I was told I lied. Did you hear him say that?"

"Yes, I did." Adele's eyes went to James. "I'm sorry, Gif."

"But it's not true!" Clara James cried.

Wolfe rasped at her, "We're all lying?"

I could have warned her, when she gave me that glance in the hall, to look out for him. Not only was she a sophisticated young woman, and not only did she glisten, but her slimness was the kind that comes from not eating enough, and Wolfe absolutely cannot stand people who don't eat enough. I knew he would be down on her from the go.

But she came back at him. "I don't mean that," she said scornfully. "Don't be so touchy! I mean I had lied to my father. What he thought about Alberto and me wasn't true. I was just bragging to him because—it doesn't matter why. Anyway, what I told him wasn't true, and I told him so that night!"

"Which night?"

"When we got home—from the stage party after *Rigoletto.* That was where my father knocked Alberto down, you know, right there on the stage. When we got home I told him that what I had said about Alberto and me wasn't true."

"When were you lying, the first time or the second?"

"Don't answer that, my dear," Judge Arnold broke in, lawyering. He looked sternly at Wolfe. "This is all irrelevant. You're welcome to the facts, but relevant facts. What Miss James told her father is immaterial."

Wolfe shook his head. "Oh no." His eyes went from right to left and back again. "Apparently I haven't made it plain. Mrs. Mion wants me to decide for her whether she has a just claim, not so much legally as morally. If it appears that Mr. James' assault on Mr. Mion was morally justified that will be a factor in my decision." He focused on Clara. "Whether my question was relevant or not, Miss James, I admit it was embarrassing and therefore invited mendacity. I withdraw it. Try this instead. Had you, prior to that stage party, given your father to understand that Mr. Mion had seduced you?"

"Well—" Clara laughed. It was a tinkly soprano laugh, rather attractive. "What a nice old-fashioned way to say it! Yes, I had. But it wasn't true!"

"But you believed it, Mr. James?"

Gifford James was having trouble holding himself in, and I concede that such leading questions about his daughter's honor from a stranger must have been hard to take. But after all it wasn't new to the rest of the audience, and anyway it sure was relevant. He forced himself to speak with quiet dignity. "I believed what my daughter told me, yes."

Wolfe nodded. "So much for that," he said in a relieved tone. "I'm glad that part is over with." His eyes moved. "Now. Mr. Grove, tell me about the conference in Mr. Mion's studio, a few hours before he died."

Rupert the Fat had his head tilted to one side, with his shrewd black eyes meeting Wolfe's. "It was for the purpose," he said in his high tenor, "of discussing the demand Mion had made for payment of damages."

"You were there?"

"I was, naturally. I was Mion's adviser and manager. Also Miss Bosley, Dr. Lloyd, Mr. James, and Judge Arnold."

"Who arranged the conference, you?"

"In a way, yes. Arnold suggested it, and I told Mion and phoned Dr. Lloyd and Miss Bosley."

"What was decided?"

"Nothing. That is, nothing definite. There was the question of the extent of the damage—how soon Mion would be able to sing again."

"What was your position?"

Grove's eyes tightened. "Didn't I say I was Mion's manager?"

"Certainly. I mean, what position did you take regarding the payment of damages?"

"I thought a preliminary payment of fifty thousand dollars should be made at once. Even if Mion's voice was soon all right he had already lost that and more. His South American tour had been canceled, and he had been unable to make a lot of records on contract, and then radio offers—"

"Nothing like fifty thousand dollars," Judge Arnold asserted aggressively. There was nothing wrong with his larynx, small as he was. "I showed figures—"

"To hell with your figures! Anybody can—"

"Please!" Wolfe rapped on his desk with a knuckle. "What was Mr. Mion's position?"

"The same as mine, of course." Grove was scowling at Arnold as he spoke to Wolfe. "We had discussed it."

"Naturally." Wolfe's eyes went left. "How did you feel about it, Mr. James?"

"I think," Arnold broke in, "that I should speak for my client. You agree, Gif?"

"Go ahead," the baritone muttered.

Arnold did, and took most of one of the three hours. I was surprised that Wolfe didn't stop him, and finally decided that he let him ramble on just to get additional support for his long-standing opinion of lawyers. If so, he got it. Arnold covered everything. He had a lot to say about tort-feasors, going back a couple of centuries, with emphasis on the mental state of a tort-feasor. Another item he covered at length was proximate cause. He got really worked up about proximate cause, but it was so involved that I lost track and passed.

Here and there, though, he made sense. At one point he said, "The idea of a preliminary payment, as they called it, was clearly inadmissible. It is not reasonable to expect a man, even if he stipulates an obligation, to make a payment thereon until either the total amount of the obligation, or an exact method of computing it, has been agreed upon."

At another point he said, "The demand for so large a sum can in fact be properly characterized as blackmail. They knew that if the action went to trial, and if we showed that my client's deed sprang from his knowledge that his daughter had been wronged, a jury would not be likely to award damages. But they also knew that we would be averse to making that defense."

"Not his knowledge," Wolfe objected. "Merely his belief. His daughter says she had misinformed him."

"We could have showed knowledge," Arnold insisted.

I looked at Clara with my brows up. She was being contradicted flatly on the chronology of her lie and her truth, but either she and her father didn't get the implication of it or they didn't want to get started on that again.

At another point Arnold said, "Even if my client's deed was tortious and damages would be collectible, the amount could not be agreed upon until the extent of the injury was known. We offered, without prejudice, twenty thousand dollars in full settlement, for a general release. They refused. They wanted a payment forthwith on account. We refused that on principle. In the end there was agreement on only one thing: that an effort should be made to arrive at the total amount of damage. Of course that was what Dr. Lloyd was there for. He was asked for a prognosis, and he stated that—but you don't need to take hearsay. He's here, and you can get it direct."

Wolfe nodded. "If you please, Doctor?"

I thought, My God, here we go again with another expert.

But Lloyd had mercy on us. He kept it down to our level and didn't take anything like an hour. Before he spoke he took another swallow from his third helping of bourbon and water with mint, which had smoothed out some of the lines on his handsome face and taken some of the worry from his eyes.

"I'll try to remember," he said slowly, "exactly what I told them. First I described the damage the blow had done. The thyroid and arytenoid cartilages on the left side had been severely injured, and to a lesser extent the cricoid." He smiled—a superior smile, but not supercilious. "I waited two weeks, using indicated treatment, thinking an operation might not be required, but it was. When I got inside I confess I was relieved; it wasn't as bad as I had feared. It was a simple operation, and he healed admirably. I wouldn't have been risking much that day if I had given assurance that his voice would be as good as ever in two months, three at the most, but the larynx is an extremely delicate instrument, and a tenor like Mion's is a remarkable phenomenon, so I was cautious enough merely to say that I would be surprised and disappointed if he wasn't ready, fully ready, for the opening of the next opera season, seven months from then. I added that my hope and expectation were actually more optimistic than that."

Lloyd pursed his lips. "That was it, I think. Nevertheless, I welcomed the suggestion that my prognosis should be reinforced by Rentner's. Apparently it would be a major factor in the decision about the amount to be paid in damages, and I didn't want the sole responsibility."

"Rentner? Who was he?" Wolfe asked.

"Dr. Abraham Rentner of Mount Sinai," Lloyd replied, in the tone I would use if someone asked me who Jackie Robinson was. "I phoned him and made an appointment for the following morning."

"I insisted on it," Rupert the Fat said importantly. "Mion had a right to collect not sometime in the distant future, but then and there. They wouldn't pay unless a total was agreed on, and if we had to name a total I wanted to be damn sure it was enough. Don't forget that that day Mion couldn't sing a note."

"He wouldn't have been able even to let out a pianissimo for at least two months," Lloyd bore him out. "I gave that as the minimum."

"There seems," Judge Arnold interposed, "to be an implication that we opposed the suggestion that a second professional opinion be secured. I must protest—"

"You did!" Grove squeaked.

"We did not!" Gifford James barked. "We merely—"

The three of them went at it, snapping and snarling. It seemed to me that they might have saved

their energy for the big issue, was anything coming to
Mrs. Mion and if so how much, but not those babies.
Their main concern was to avoid the slightest risk of
agreeing on anything at all. Wolfe patiently let them
get where they were headed for—nowhere—and then
invited a new voice in. He turned to Adele and spoke.

"Miss Bosley, we haven't heard from you. Which
side were you on?"

IV

Adele Bosley had been sitting taking it in, sipping
occasionally at her rum collins—now her second one—
and looking, I thought, pretty damn intelligent.
Though it was the middle of August, she was the only
one of the six who had a really good tan. Her public
relations with the sun were excellent.

She shook her head. "I wasn't on either side, Mr.
Wolfe. My only interest was that of my employer, the
Metropolitan Opera Association. Naturally we wanted
it settled privately, without any scandal. I had no opinion whatever on whether—on the point at issue."

"And expressed none?"

"No. I merely urged them to get it settled if possible."

"Fair enough!" Clara James blurted. It was a
sneer. "You might have helped my father a little, since
he got your job for you. Or had you—"

"Be quiet, Clara!" James told her with authority.

But she ignored him and finished it. "Or had you
already paid in full for that?"

I was shocked. Judge Arnold looked pained. Rupert
the Fat giggled. Doc Lloyd took a gulp of bourbon and
water.

In view of the mildly friendly attitude I was developing toward Adele I sort of hoped she would throw something at the slim and glistening Miss James, but all she did was appeal to the father. "Can't you handle the brat, Gif?"

Then, without waiting for an answer, she turned to Wolfe. "Miss James likes to use her imagination. What she implied is not on the record. Not anybody's record."

Wolfe nodded. "It wouldn't belong on this one anyhow." He made a face. "To go back to relevancies, what time did that conference break up?"

"Why—Mr. James and Judge Arnold left first, around four-thirty. Then Dr. Lloyd, soon after. I stayed a few minutes with Mion and Mr. Grove, and then went."

"Where did you go?"

"To my office, on Broadway."

"How long did you stay at your office?"

She looked surprised. "I don't know—yes, I do too, of course. Until a little after seven. I had things to do, and I typed a confidential report of the conference at Mion's."

"Did you see Mion again before he died? Or phone him?"

"See him?" She was more surprised. "How could I? Don't you know he was found dead at seven o'clock? That was before I left the office."

"Did you phone him? Between four-thirty and seven?"

"No." Adele was puzzled and slightly exasperated. It struck me that Wolfe was recklessly getting onto thin ice, mighty close to the forbidden subject of murder. Adele added, "I don't know what you're getting at."

"Neither do I," Judge Arnold put in with emphasis. He smiled sarcastically. "Unless it's force of habit with you, asking people where they were at the time a death by violence occurred. Why don't you go after all of us?"

"That's what I intend to do," Wolfe said imperturbably. "I would like to know why Mion decided to kill himself, because that has a bearing on the opinion I shall give his widow. I understand that two or three of you have said that he was wrought up when that conference ended, but not despondent or splenetic. I know he committed suicide; the police can't be flummoxed on a thing like that; but why?"

"I doubt," Adele Bosley offered, "if you know how a singer—especially a great artist like Mion—how he feels when he can't let a sound out, when he can't even talk except in an undertone or a whisper. It's horrible."

"Anyway, you never knew with him," Rupert Grove contributed. "In rehearsal I've heard him do an aria like an angel and then rush out weeping because he thought he had slurred a release. One minute he was up in the sky and the next he was under a rug."

Wolfe grunted. "Nevertheless, anything said to him by anyone during the two hours preceding his suicide is pertinent to this inquiry, to establish Mrs. Mion's moral position. I want to know where you people were that day, after the conference up to seven o'clock, and what you did."

"My God!" Judge Arnold threw up his hands. The hands came down again. "All right, it's getting late. As Miss Bosley told you, my client and I left Mion's studio together. We went to the Churchill bar and drank and talked. A little later Miss James joined us, stayed long enough for a drink, I suppose half an hour, and left. Mr. James and I remained together until after seven. During that time neither of us communicated with Mion, nor arranged for anyone else to. I believe that covers it?"

"Thank you," Wolfe said politely. "You corroborate, of course, Mr. James?"

"I do," the baritone said gruffly. "This is a lot of goddam nonsense."

"It does begin to sound like it," Wolfe conceded. "Dr. Lloyd? If you don't mind?"

He hadn't better, since he had been mellowed by four ample helpings of our best bourbon, and he didn't. "Not at all," he said cooperatively. "I made calls on five patients, two on upper Fifth Avenue, one in the East Sixties, and two at the hospital. I got home a little after six and had just finished dressing after taking a bath when Fred Weppler phoned me about Mion. Of course I went at once."

"You hadn't seen Mion or phoned him?"

"Not since I left after the conference. Perhaps I should have, but I had no idea—I'm not a psychiatrist, but I was his doctor."

"He was mercurial, was he?"

"Yes, he was." Lloyd pursed his lips. "Of course, that's not a medical term."

"Far from it," Wolfe agreed. He shifted his gaze. "Mr. Grove, I don't have to ask you if you phoned Mion, since it is on record that you did. Around five o'clock?"

Rupert the Fat had his head tilted again. Apparently that was his favorite pose for conversing. He corrected Wolfe. "It was after five. More like a quarter past."

"Where did you phone from?"

"The Harvard Club."

I thought, I'll be damned, it takes all kinds to make a Harvard Club.

"What was said?"

"Not much." Grove's lips twisted. "It's none of your damn business, you know, but the others have obliged, and I'll string along. I had forgotten to ask him if he would endorse a certain product for a thousand dollars, and the agency wanted an answer. We talked less than five minutes. First he said he wouldn't and then he said he would. That was all."

"Did he sound like a man getting ready to kill himself?"

"Not the slightest. He was glum, but naturally, since he couldn't sing and couldn't expect to for at least two months."

"After you phoned Mion what did you do?"

"I stayed at the club. I ate dinner there and hadn't quite finished when the news came that Mion had killed himself. So I'm still behind that ice cream and coffee."

"That's too bad. When you phoned Mion, did you again try to persuade him not to press his claim against Mr. James?"

Grove's head straightened up. "Did I what?" he demanded.

"You heard me," Wolfe said rudely. "What's surprising about it? Naturally Mrs. Mion has informed me, since I'm working for her. You were opposed to Mion's asking for payment in the first place and tried to talk him out of it. You said the publicity would be so harmful that it wasn't worth it. He demanded that you support the claim and threatened to cancel your contract if you refused. Isn't that correct?"

"It is not." Grove's black eyes were blazing. "It wasn't like that at all! I merely gave him my opinion.

When it was decided to make the claim I went along."
His voice went up a notch higher, though I wouldn't
have thought it possible. "I certainly did!"

"I see." Wolfe wasn't arguing. "What is your opinion now, about Mrs. Mion's claim?"

"I don't think she has one. I don't believe she can
collect. If I were in James' place I certainly wouldn't
pay her a cent."

Wolfe nodded. "You don't like her, do you?"

"Frankly, I don't. No. I never have. Do I have to
like her?"

"No, indeed. Especially since she doesn't like you
either." Wolfe shifted in his chair and leaned back. I
could tell from the line of his lips, straightened out,
that the next item on the agenda was one he didn't
care for, and I understood why when I saw his eyes
level at Clara James. I'll bet that if he had known that
he would have to be dealing with that type he wouldn't
have taken the job. He spoke to her testily. "Miss
James, you've heard what has been said?"

"I was wondering," she complained, as if she had
been holding in a grievance, "if you were going to go on
ignoring me. I was around too, you know."

"I know. I haven't forgotten you." His tone implied
that he only wished he could. "When you had a drink in
the Churchill bar with your father and Judge Arnold,
why did they send you up to Mion's studio to see him?
What for?"

Arnold and James protested at once, loudly and simultaneously. Wolfe, paying no attention to them,
waited to hear Clara, her voice having been drowned
by theirs.

". . . nothing to do with it," she was finishing. "I
sent myself."

"It was your own idea?"

"Entirely. I have one once in a while, all alone."

"What did you go for?"

"You don't need to answer, my dear," Arnold told her.

She ignored him. "They told me what had happened at the conference, and I was mad. I thought it was a holdup—but I wasn't going to tell Alberto that. I thought I could talk him out of it."

"You went to appeal to him for old times' sake?"

She looked pleased. "You have the nicest way of putting things! Imagine a girl my age having old times!"

"I'm glad you like my diction, Miss James." Wolfe was furious. "Anyhow, you went. Arriving at a quarter past six?"

"Just about, yes."

"Did you see Mion?"

"No."

"Why not?"

"He wasn't there. At least—" She stopped. Her eyes weren't glistening quite so much. She went on, "That's what I thought then. I went to the thirteenth floor and rang the bell at the door to the studio. It's a loud bell—he had it loud to be heard above his voice and the piano when he was practicing—but I couldn't hear it from the hall because the door is soundproofed too, and after I had pushed the button a few times I wasn't sure the bell was ringing so I knocked on the door. I like to finish anything I start, and I thought he must be there, so I rang the bell some more and took off my shoe and pounded on the door with the heel. Then I went down to the twelfth floor by the public stairs and rang the bell at the apartment door. That was really stupid, because I know how Mrs. Mion hates me, but anyway I did. She came to the door and said she thought Alberto was up in the studio, and I said he wasn't, and she shut the door in my face. I went home and mixed myself a drink—which reminds me, I must admit this is good scotch, though I never heard of it before."

She lifted her glass and jiggled it to swirl the ice. "Any questions?"

"No," Wolfe growled. He glanced at the clock on the wall and then along the line of faces. "I shall certainly report to Mrs. Mion," he told them, "that you were not grudging with the facts."

"And what else?" Arnold inquired.

"I don't know. We'll see."

That they didn't like. I wouldn't have supposed anyone could name a subject on which those six characters would have been in unanimous accord, but Wolfe turned the trick in five words. They wanted a verdict; failing that, an opinion; failing that, at least a hint. Adele Bosley was stubborn, Rupert the Fat was so indignant he squeaked, and Judge Arnold was next door to nasty. Wolfe was patient up to a point, but finally stood up and told them good night as if he meant it. The note it ended on was such that before going not one of them shelled out a word of appreciation for all the refreshment, not even Adele, the expert on public relations, or Doc Lloyd, who had practically emptied the bourbon bottle.

With the front door locked and bolted for the night, I returned to the office. To my astonishment Wolfe was still on his feet, standing over by the bookshelves, glaring at the backbones.

"Restless?" I asked courteously.

He turned and said aggressively, "I want another bottle of beer."

"Nuts. You've had five since dinner." I didn't

bother to put much feeling into it, as the routine was familiar. He had himself set the quota of five bottles between dinner and bedtime, and usually stuck to it, but when anything sent his humor far enough down he liked to shift the responsibility so he could be sore at me too.

It was just part of my job. "Nothing doing," I said firmly. "I counted 'em. Five. What's the trouble, a whole evening gone and still no murderer?"

"Bah." He compressed his lips. "That's not it. If that were all we could close it up before going to bed. It's that confounded gun with wings." He gazed at me with his eyes narrowed, as if suspecting that I had wings too. "I could, of course, just ignore it— No. No, in view of the state our clients are in, it would be fool-hardy. We'll have to clear it up. There's no alternative."

"That's a nuisance. Can I help any?"

"Yes. Phone Mr. Cramer first thing in the morning. Ask him to be here at eleven o'clock."

My brows went up. "But he's interested only in homicides. Do I tell him we've got one to show him?"

"No. Tell him I guarantee that it's worth the trouble." Wolfe took a step toward me. "Archie."

"Yes, sir."

"I've had a bad evening and I'll have another bottle."

"You will not. Not a chance." Fritz had come in and we were starting to clear up. "It's after midnight and you're in the way. Go to bed."

"One wouldn't hurt him," Fritz muttered.

"You're a help," I said bitterly. "I warn both of you, I've got a gun in my pocket. What a household!"

V

For nine months of the year Inspector Cramer of Homicide, big and broad and turning gray, looked the part well enough, but in the summertime the heat kept his face so red that he was a little gaudy. He knew it and didn't like it, and as a result he was some harder to deal with in August than in January. If an occasion arises for me to commit a murder in Manhattan I hope it will be winter.

Tuesday at noon he sat in the red leather chair and looked at Wolfe with no geniality. Detained by another appointment, he hadn't been able to make it at eleven, the hour when Wolfe adjourns the morning session with his orchids up in the plant rooms. Wolfe wasn't exactly beaming either, and I was looking forward to some vaudeville. Also I was curious to see how Wolfe would go about getting dope on a murder from Cramer without spilling it that there had been one, as Cramer was by no means a nitwit.

"I'm on my way uptown," Cramer grumbled, "and haven't got much time."

That was probably a barefaced lie. He merely didn't want to admit that an inspector of the NYPD would call on a private detective on request, even though it was Nero Wolfe and I had told him we had something hot.

"What is it," he grumbled on, "the Dickinson thing? Who brought you in?"

Wolfe shook his head. "No one, thank heaven. It's about the murder of Alberto Mion."

I goggled at him. This was away beyond me. Right off he had let the dog loose, when I had thought the whole point was that there was no dog on the place.

"Mion?" Cramer wasn't interested. "Not one of mine."

"It soon will be. Alberto Mion, the famous opera singer. Four months ago, on April nineteenth. In his studio on East End Avenue. Shot—"

"Oh." Cramer nodded. "Yeah, I remember. But you're stretching it a little. It was suicide."

"No. It was first-degree murder."

Cramer regarded him for three breaths. Then, in no hurry, he got a cigar from his pocket, inspected it, and stuck it in his mouth. In a moment he took it out again.

"I have never known it to fail," he remarked, "that you can be counted on for a headache. Who says it was murder?"

"I have reached that conclusion."

"Then that's settled." Cramer's sarcasm was usually a little heavy. "Have you bothered any about evidence?"

"I have none."

"Good. Evidence just clutters a murder up." Cramer stuck the cigar back in his mouth and exploded, "When did you start keeping your sentences so goddam short? Go ahead and talk!"

"Well—" Wolfe considered. "It's a little difficult. You're probably not familiar with the details, since it was so long ago and was recorded as suicide."

"I remember it fairly well. As you say, he was famous. Go right ahead."

Wolfe leaned back and closed his eyes. "Interrupt me if you need to. I had six people here for a talk last evening." He pronounced their names and identified them. "Five of them were present at a conference in Mion's studio which ended two hours before he was found dead. The sixth, Miss James, banged on the studio door at a quarter past six and got no reply, presumably because he was dead then. My conclusion that Mion was murdered is based on things I have heard said. I'm not going to repeat them to you—because it would take too long, because it's a question of emphasis and interpretation, and because you have already heard them."

"I wasn't here last evening," Cramer said dryly.

"So you weren't. Instead of 'you,' I should have said the Police Department. It must all be in the files. They were questioned at the time it happened, and told their stories as they have now told them to me. You can get it there. Have you ever known me to have to eat my words?"

"I've seen times when I would have liked to shove them down your throat."

"But you never have. Here are three more I shall not eat: Mion was murdered. I won't tell you, now, how I reached that conclusion; study your files."

Cramer was keeping himself under restraint. "I don't have to study them," he declared, "for one detail —how he was killed. Are you saying he fired the gun himself but was driven to it?"

"No. The murderer fired the gun."

"It must have been quite a murderer. It's quite a trick to pry a guy's mouth open and stick a gun in it without getting bit. Would you mind naming him?"

Wolfe shook his head. "I haven't got that far yet. But it isn't the objection you raise that's bothering me; that can be overcome; it's something else." He leaned forward and was earnest. "Look here, Mr. Cramer. It would not have been impossible for me to see this through alone, deliver the murderer and the evidence to you, and flap my wings and crow. But first, I have no ambition to expose you as a zany, since you're not; and second, I need your help. I am not now prepared to prove to you that Mion was murdered; I can only assure you that he was and repeat that I won't have to eat it—and neither will you. Isn't that enough, at least to arouse your interest?"

Cramer stopped chewing the cigar. He never lit one. "Sure," he said grimly. "Hell, I'm interested. Another first-class headache. I'm flattered you want me to help. How?"

"I want you to arrest two people as material witnesses, question them, and let them out on bail."

"Which two? Why not all six?" I warned you his sarcasm was hefty.

"But"—Wolfe ignored it—"under clearly defined conditions. They must not know that I am responsible; they must not even know that I have spoken with you. The arrests should be made late this afternoon or early evening, so they'll be kept in custody all night and until they arrange for bail in the morning. The bail need not be high; that's not important. The questioning should be fairly prolonged and severe, not merely a gesture, and if they get little or no sleep so much the better. Of course this sort of thing is routine for you."

"Yeah, we do it constantly." Cramer's tone was unchanged. "But when we ask for a warrant we like to have a fairly good excuse. We wouldn't like to put down that it's to do Nero Wolfe a favor. I don't want to be contrary."

"There's ample excuse for these two. They *are* material witnesses. They are indeed."

"You haven't named them. Who are they?"

"The man and woman who found the body. Mr. Frederick Weppler, the music critic, and Mrs. Mion, the widow."

This time I didn't goggle, but I had to catch myself

quick. It was a first if there ever was one. Time and again I have seen Wolfe go far, on a few occasions much too far, to keep a client from being pinched. He regards it as an unbearable personal insult. And here he was, practically begging the law to haul Fred and Peggy in, when I had deposited her check for five grand only the day before!

"Oh," Cramer said. "Them?"

"Yes, sir," Wolfe assured him cooperatively. "As you know or can learn from the files, there is plenty to ask them about it. Mr. Weppler was there for lunch that day, with others, and when the others left he remained with Mrs. Mion. What was discussed? What did they do that afternoon; where were they? Why did Mr. Weppler return to the Mion apartment at seven o'clock? Why did he and Mrs. Mion ascend together to the studio? After finding the body, why did Mr. Weppler go downstairs before notifying the police, to get a list of names from the doorman and elevator man? An extraordinary performance. Was it Mion's habit to take an afternoon nap? Did he sleep with his mouth open?"

"Much obliged," Cramer said not gratefully. "You're a wonder at thinking of questions to ask. But even if Mion did take naps with his mouth open, I doubt if he did it standing up. And after the bullet left his head it went up to the ceiling, as I remember it. Now." Cramer put his palms on the arms of the chair, with the cigar in his mouth tilted up at about the angle the gun in Mion's mouth had probably been. "Who's your client?"

"No," Wolfe said regretfully. "I'm not ready to disclose that."

"I thought not. In fact, there isn't one single damn thing you have disclosed. You've got no evidence, or if you have any you're keeping it under your belt. You've got a conclusion you like, that will help a client you won't name, and you want me to test it for you by arresting two reputable citizens and giving them the works. I've seen samples of your nerve before, but this is tops. For God's sake!"

"I've told you I won't eat it, and neither will you. If—"

"You'd eat one of your own orchids if you had to earn a fee!"

That started the fireworks. I have sat many times and listened to that pair in a slugging match and enjoyed every minute of it, but this one got so hot that I wasn't exactly sure I was enjoying it. At 12:40 Cramer was on his feet, starting to leave. At 12:45 he was back in the red leather chair, shaking his fist and snarling. At 12:48 Wolfe was leaning back with his eyes shut, pretending he was deaf. At 12:52 he was pounding his desk and bellowing.

At ten past one it was all over. Cramer had taken it and was gone. He had made a condition, that there would first be a check of the record and a staff talk, but that didn't matter, since the arrests were to be postponed until after judges had gone home. He accepted the proviso that the victims were not to know that Wolfe had a hand in it, so it could have been said that he was knuckling under, but actually he was merely using horse sense. No matter how much he discounted Wolfe's three words that were not to be eaten—and he knew from experience how risky it was to discount Wolfe just for the hell of it—they made it fairly probable that it wouldn't hurt to give Mion's death another look; and in that case a session with the couple who had found the body was as good a way to start as any. As a matter of fact, the only detail that Cramer choked on was Wolfe's refusal to tell who his client was.

As I followed Wolfe into the dining room for lunch I remarked to his outspread back, "There are already eight hundred and nine people in the metropolitan area who would like to poison you. This will make it eight hundred and eleven. Don't think they won't find out sooner or later."

"Of course they will," he conceded, pulling his chair back. "But too late."

The rest of that day and evening nothing happened at all, as far as we knew.

VI

I was at my desk in the office at 10:40 the next morning when the phone rang. I got it and told the transmitter, "Nero Wolfe's office, Archie Goodwin speaking."

"I want to talk to Mr. Wolfe."

"He won't be available until eleven o'clock. Can I help?"

"This is urgent. This is Weppler, Frederick Weppler. I'm in a booth in a drugstore on Ninth Avenue near Twentieth Street. Mrs. Mion is with me. We've been arrested."

"Good God!" I was horrified. "What for?"

"To ask us about Mion's death. They had material-witness warrants. They kept us all night, and we just got out on bail. I had a lawyer arrange for the bail, but I don't want him to know about—that we consulted Wolfe, and he's not with us. We want to see Wolfe."

"You sure do," I agreed emphatically. "It's a damn outrage. Come on up here. He'll be down from the plant rooms by the time you arrive. Grab a taxi."

"We can't. That's why I'm phoning. We're being followed by two detectives and we don't want them to know we're seeing Wolfe. How can we shake them?"

It would have saved time and energy to tell him to come ahead, that a couple of official tails needn't worry him, but I thought I'd better play along.

"For God's sake," I said, disgusted. "Cops give me a pain in the neck. Listen. Are you listening?"

"Yes."

"Go to the Feder Paper Company, Five-thirty-five West Seventeenth Street. In the office ask for Mr. Sol Feder. Tell him your name is Montgomery. He'll conduct you along a passage that exits on Eighteenth Street. Right there, either at the curb or double-parked, will be a taxi with a handkerchief on the door handle. I'll be in it. Don't lose any time climbing in. Have you got it?"

"I think so. You'd better repeat the address."

I did so, and told him to wait ten minutes before starting, to give me time to get there. Then, after hanging up, I phoned Sol Feder to instruct him, got Wolfe on the house phone to inform him, and beat it.

I should have told him to wait fifteen or twenty minutes instead of ten, because I got to my post on Eighteenth Street barely in time. My taxi had just stopped, and I was reaching out to tie my handkerchief on the door handle, when here they came across the sidewalk like a bat out of hell. I swung the door wide, and Fred practically threw Peggy in and dived in after her.

"Okay, driver," I said sternly, "you know where," and we rolled.

As we swung into Tenth Avenue I asked if they had had breakfast and they said yes, not with any enthusiasm. The fact is, they looked as if they were entirely out of enthusiasm. Peggy's lightweight green jacket, which she had on over a tan cotton dress, was rumpled and not very clean, and her face looked neglected. Fred's hair might not have been combed for a month, and his brown tropical worsted was anything but natty. They sat holding hands, and about once a minute Fred twisted around to look through the rear window.

"We're loose all right," I assured him. "I've been saving Sol Feder just for an emergency like this."

It was only a five-minute ride. When I ushered them into the office Wolfe was there in his big custom-made chair behind his desk. He arose to greet them, invited them to sit, asked if they had breakfasted properly, and said that the news of their arrest had been an unpleasant shock.

"One thing," Fred blurted, still standing. "We came to see you and consult you in confidence, and forty-eight hours later we were arrested. Was that pure coincidence?"

Wolfe finished getting himself re-established in his chair. "That won't help us any, Mr. Weppler," he said without resentment. "If that's your frame of mind you'd better go somewhere and cool off. You and Mrs. Mion are my clients. An insinuation that I am capable of acting against the interest of a client is too childish for discussion. What did the police ask you about?"

But Fred wasn't satisfied. "You're not a double-crosser," he conceded. "I know that. But what about Goodwin here? He may not be a double-crosser either, but he might have got careless in conversation with someone."

Wolfe's eyes moved. "Archie. Did you?"

"No, sir. But he can postpone asking my pardon. They've had a hard night." I looked at Fred. "Sit down and relax. If I had a careless tongue I wouldn't last at this job a week."

"It's damn funny," Fred persisted. He sat. "Mrs. Mion agrees with me. Don't you, Peggy?"

Peggy, in the red leather chair, gave him a glance and then looked back at Wolfe. "I did, I guess," she confessed. "Yes, I did. But now that I'm here, seeing you—" She made a gesture. "Oh, forget it! There's no one else to go to. We know lawyers, of course, but we don't want to tell a lawyer what we know—about the gun. We've already told you. But now the police suspect something, and we're out on bail, and you've got to do something!"

"What did you find out Monday evening?" Fred demanded. "You stalled when I phoned yesterday. What did they say?"

"They recited facts," Wolfe replied. "As I told you on the phone, I made some progress. I have nothing to add to that—now. But I want to know, I *must* know, what line the police took with you. Did they know what you told me about the gun?"

They both said no.

Wolfe grunted. "Then I might reasonably ask that you withdraw your insinuation that I or Mr. Goodwin betrayed you. What did they ask about?"

The answers to that took a good half an hour. The cops hadn't missed a thing that was included in the picture as they knew it, and, with instructions from Cramer to make it thorough, they hadn't left a scrap. Far from limiting it to the day of Mion's death, they had been particularly curious about Peggy's and Fred's feelings and actions during the months both prior and subsequent thereto. Several times I had to take the tip of my tongue between my teeth to keep from asking the clients why they hadn't told the cops to go soak their heads, but I really knew why: they had been scared. A scared man is only half a man. By the time they finished reporting on their ordeal I was feeling sympathetic, and even guilty on behalf of Wolfe, when suddenly he snapped me out of it.

He sat a while tapping the arm of his chair with a fingertip, and then looked at me and said abruptly, "Archie. Draw a check to the order of Mrs. Mion for five thousand dollars."

They gawked at him. I got up and headed for the safe. They demanded to know what the idea was. I stood at the safe door to listen.

"I'm quitting," Wolfe said curtly. "I can't stand you. I told you Sunday that one or both of you were lying, and you stubbornly denied it. I undertook to work around your lie, and I did my best. But now that the police have got curious about Mion's death, and specifically about you, I refuse longer to risk it. I am willing to be a Quixote, but not a chump. In breaking with you, I should tell you that I shall immediately inform Inspector Cramer of all that you have told me. If, when the police start the next round with you, you are fools enough to contradict me, heaven knows what will happen. Your best course will be to acknowledge the truth and let them pursue the investigation you hired me for; but I would also warn you that they are not simpletons and they too will know that you are lying—at least one of you. Archie, what are you standing there gaping for? Get the checkbook."

I opened the safe door.

Neither of them had uttered a peep. I suppose they were too tired to react normally. As I returned to my desk they just sat, looking at each other. As I started making the entry on the stub, Fred's voice came.

"You can't do this. This isn't ethical."

"Pfui." Wolfe snorted. "You hire me to get you out of a fix, and lie to me about it, and talk of ethics! Incidentally, I did make progress Monday evening. I cleared everything up but two details, but the devil of it is that one of them depends on you. I have got to know who put that gun on the floor beside the body. I am convinced that it was one of you, but you won't admit it. So I'm helpless and that's a pity, because I am also convinced that neither of you was involved in Mion's death. If there were—"

"What's that?" Fred demanded. There was nothing wrong with his reaction now. "You're convinced that neither of us was involved?"

"I am."

Fred was out of his chair. He went to Wolfe's desk, put his palms on it, leaned forward, and said harshly, "Do you mean that? Look at me. Open your eyes and look at me! Do you mean that?"

"Yes," Wolfe told him. "Certainly I mean it."

Fred gazed at him another moment and then straightened up. "All right," he said, the harshness gone. "I put the gun on the floor."

A wail came from Peggy. She sailed out of her chair and to him and seized his arm with both hands. "Fred! No! Fred!" she pleaded. I wouldn't have thought her capable of wailing, but of course she was tired to begin with. He put a hand on top of hers and then decided that was inadequate and took her in his arms. For a minute he concentrated on her. Finally he turned his face to Wolfe and spoke.

"I may regret this, but if I do you will too. By God, you will." He was quite positive of it. "All right, I lied. I put the gun on the floor. Now it's up to you." He held the other client closer. "I did, Peggy. Don't say I should have told you—maybe I should—but I couldn't. It'll be all right, dearest, really it will—"

"Sit down," Wolfe said crossly. After a moment he made it an order. "Confound it, sit down!"

Peggy freed herself, Fred letting her go, and returned to her chair and dropped into it. Fred perched on its arm, with a hand on her far shoulder, and she put her hand up to his. Their eyes, suspicious, afraid, defiant, and hopeful all at once, were on Wolfe.

He stayed cross. "I assume," he said, "that you see how it is. You haven't impressed me. I already knew one of you had put the gun there. How could anyone else have entered the studio during those few minutes? The truth you have told me will be worse than useless, it will be extremely dangerous, unless you follow it with more truth. Try another lie and there's no telling what will happen; I might not be able to save you. Where did you find it?"

"Don't worry," Fred said quietly. "You've screwed it out of me and you'll get it straight. When we went in and found the body I saw the gun where Mion always kept it, on the base of Caruso's bust. Mrs. Mion didn't see it; she didn't look that way. When I left her in her bedroom I went back up. I picked the gun up by the trigger guard and smelled it; it had been fired. I put it on the floor by the body, returned to the apartment, went out, and took the elevator to the ground floor. The rest was just as I told you Sunday."

Wolfe grunted. "You may have been in love, but you didn't think much of her intelligence. You assumed that after killing him she hadn't had the wit to leave the gun where he might have dropped—"

"I did not, damn you!"

"Nonsense. Of course you did. Who else would you have wanted to shield? And afterward it got you in a pickle. When you had to agree with her that the gun hadn't been there when you and she entered, you were hobbled. You didn't dare tell her what you had done because of the implication that you suspected her, especially when she seemed to be suspecting you. You couldn't be sure whether she really did suspect you, or whether she was only—"

"I never did suspect him," Peggy said firmly. It was a job to make her voice firm, but she managed it. "And he never suspected me, not really. We just weren't sure—sure all the way down—and when you're in love and want it to last you've got to be sure."

"That was it," Fred agreed. They were looking at each other. "That was it exactly."

"All right, I'll take this," Wolfe said curtly. "I think you've told the truth, Mr. Weppler."

"I know damn well I have."

Wolfe nodded. "You sound like it. I have a good ear for the truth. Now take Mrs. Mion home. I've got to work, but first I must think it over. As I said, there were two details, and you've disposed of only one. You can't help with the other. Go home and eat something."

"Who wants to eat?" Fred demanded fiercely. "We want to know what you're going to do!"

"I've got to brush my teeth," Peggy stated. I shot her a glance of admiration and affection. Women's saying things like that at times like that is one of the reasons I enjoy their company. No man alive, under those circumstances, would have felt that he had to brush his teeth and said so.

Besides, it made it easier to get rid of them without being rude. Fred tried to insist that they had a right to know what the program was, and to help consider the prospects, but was finally compelled to accept Wolfe's mandate that when a man hired an expert the only authority he kept was the right to fire. That, combined with Peggy's longing for a toothbrush and Wolfe's assurance that he would keep them informed, got them on their way without a ruckus.

When, after letting them out, I returned to the office, Wolfe was drumming on his desk blotter with a paperknife, scowling at it, though I had told him a hundred times that it ruined the blotter. I went and got the checkbook and replaced it in the safe, having put nothing on the stub but the date, so no harm was done.

"Twenty minutes till lunch," I announced, swiveling my chair and sitting. "Will that be enough to hogtie the second detail?"

No reply.

I refused to be sensitive. "If you don't mind," I inquired pleasantly, "what is the second detail?"

Again no reply, but after a moment he dropped the paperknife, leaned back, and sighed clear down.

"That confounded gun," he growled. "How did it get from the floor to the bust? Who moved it?"

I stared at him. "My God," I complained, "you're hard to satisfy. You've just had two clients arrested and worked like a dog, getting the gun from the bust to the floor. Now you want to get it from the floor to the bust again? What the hell!"

"Not again. Prior to."

"Prior to what?"

"To the discovery of the body." His eyes slanted at me. "What do you think of this? A man—or a woman, no matter which—entered the studio and killed Mion in a manner that would convey a strong presumption of suicide. He deliberately planned it that way: it's not as difficult as the traditional police theory assumes. Then he placed the gun on the base of the bust, twenty feet away from the body, and departed. What do you think of it?"

"I don't think; I know. It didn't happen that way, unless he suddenly went batty after he pulled the trigger, which seems far-fetched."

"Precisely. Having planned it to look like suicide, he placed the gun on the floor near the body. That is not discussible. But Mr. Weppler found it on the bust. Who took it from the floor and put it there, and when and why?"

"Yeah." I scratched my nose. "That's annoying. I'll admit the question is relevant and material, but why the hell do you let it in? Why don't you let it lay? Get him or her pinched, indicted, and tried. The cops will testify that the gun was there on the floor, and that will suit the jury fine, since it was framed for suicide. Verdict, provided you've sewed up things like motive and opportunity, guilty." I waved a hand. "Simple. Why bring it up at all about the gun being so fidgety?"

Wolfe grunted. "The clients. I have to earn my fee. They want their minds cleared, and they know the gun wasn't on the floor when they discovered the body. For the jury, I can't leave it that the gun was on the bust, and for the clients I can't leave it that it stayed on the floor where the murderer put it. Having, through Mr. Weppler, got it from the bust to the floor, I must now go back and get it from the floor to the bust. You see that?"

"Only too plain." I whistled for help. "I'll be damned. How're you coming on?"

"I've just started." He sat up straight. "But I must clear my own mind, for lunch. Please hand me Mr. Shanks's orchid catalogue."

That was all for the moment, and during meals Wolfe excludes business not only from the conversation but also from the air. After lunch he returned to the office and got comfortable in his chair. For a while he just sat, and then began pushing his lips out and in, and I knew he was doing hard labor. Having no idea how he proposed to move the gun from the floor to the bust, I was wondering how long it might take, and whether he would have to get Cramer to arrest someone else, and if so who. I have seen him sit there like that, working for hours on end, but this time twenty minutes did it. It wasn't three o'clock yet when he pronounced my name gruffly and opened his eyes.

"Archie."

"Yes, sir."

"I can't do this. You'll have to."

"You mean dope it? I'm sorry, I'm busy."

"I mean execute it." He made a face. "I will not undertake to handle that young woman. It would be an ordeal, and I might botch it. It's just the thing for you. Your notebook. I'll dictate a document and then we'll discuss it."

"Yes, sir. I wouldn't call Miss Bosley really young."

"Not Miss Bosley. Miss James."

"Oh." I got the notebook.

VII

At a quarter past four, Wolfe having gone up to the plant rooms for his afternoon session with the orchids, I sat at my desk, glowering at the phone, feeling the way I imagine Jackie Robinson feels when he strikes out with the bases full. I had phoned Clara James to ask her to come for a ride with me in the convertible, and she had pushed my nose in.

If that sounds as if I like myself beyond reason, not

so. I am quite aware that I bat close to a thousand on invitations to damsels only because I don't issue one unless the circumstances strongly indicate that it will be accepted. But that has got me accustomed to hearing yes, and therefore it was a rude shock to listen to her unqualified no. Besides, I had taken the trouble to go upstairs and change to a Pillater shirt and a tropical worsted made by Corley, and there I was, all dressed up.

I concocted three schemes and rejected them, concocted a fourth and bought it, reached for the phone, and dialed the number again. Clara's voice answered, as it had before. As soon as she learned who it was she got impatient.

"I told you I had a cocktail date! Please don't—"

"Hold it," I told her bluntly. "I made a mistake. I was being kind. I wanted to get you out into the nice open air before I told you the bad news. I—"

"What bad news?"

"A woman just told Mr. Wolfe and me that there are five people besides her, and maybe more, who know that you had a key to Alberto Mion's studio door."

Silence. Sometimes silences irritate me, but I didn't mind this one. Finally her voice came, totally different. "It's a silly lie. Who told you?"

"I forget. And I'm not discussing it on the phone. Two things and two only. First, if this gets around, what about your banging on the door for ten minutes, trying to get in, while he was in there dead? When you had a key? It would make even a cop skeptical. Second, meet me at the Churchill bar at five sharp and we'll talk it over. Yes or no."

"But this is so—you're so—"

"Hold it. No good. Yes or no."

Another silence, shorter, and then, "Yes," and she hung up.

I never keep a woman waiting and saw no reason to make an exception of this one, so I got to the Churchill bar eight minutes ahead of time. It was spacious, air-conditioned, well-fitted in all respects, and even in the middle of August well-fitted also in the matter of customers, male and female. I strolled through, glancing around but not expecting her yet, and was surprised when I heard my name and saw her in a booth. Of course she hadn't had far to come, but even so she had wasted no time. She already had a drink and it was nearly gone. I joined her and immediately a waiter was there.

"You're having?" I asked her.

"Scotch on the rocks."

I told the waiter to bring two and he went.

She leaned forward at me and began in a breath, "Listen, this is absolutely silly, you just tell me who told you that, why, it's absolutely crazy—"

"Wait a minute." I stopped her more with my eyes than my words. Hers were glistening at me. "That's not the way to start, because it won't get us anywhere." I got a paper from my pocket and unfolded it. It was a neatly typed copy of the document Wolfe had dictated. "The quickest and easiest way will be for you to read this first, then you'll know what it's about."

I handed her the paper. You might as well read it while she does. It was dated that day:

I, Clara James, hereby declare that on Tuesday, April 19, I entered the apartment house at 620 East End Avenue, New York City, at or about 6:15 P.M., and took the elevator to the 13th floor. I rang the bell at the door of the studio of

Alberto Mion. No one came to the door and
there was no sound from within. The door was
not quite closed. It was not open enough to
show a crack, but was not latched or locked.
After ringing again and getting no response, I
opened the door and entered.

Alberto Mion's body was lying on the floor
over near the piano. He was dead. There was a
hole in the top of his head. There was no question whether he was dead. I got dizzy and had to
sit down on the floor and put my head down to
keep from fainting. I didn't touch the body.
There was a revolver there on the floor, not far
from the body, and I picked it up. I think I sat
on the floor about five minutes, but it might
have been a little more or less. When I got back
on my feet and started for the door I became
aware that the revolver was still in my hand. I
placed it on the base of the bust of Caruso.
Later I realized I shouldn't have done that, but
at the time I was too shocked and dazed to know
what I was doing.

I left the studio, pulling the door shut behind
me, went down the public stairs to the twelfth
floor, and rang the bell at the door of the Mion
apartment. I intended to tell Mrs. Mion about it,
but when she appeared there in the doorway it
was impossible to get it out. I couldn't tell her
that her husband was up in the studio, dead.
Later I regretted this, but I now see no reason
to regret it or apologize for it, and I simply
could not get the words out. I said I had wanted
to see her husband, and had rung the bell at the
studio and no one had answered. Then I rang

for the elevator and went down to the street and went home.

Having been unable to tell Mrs. Mion, I told no one. I would have told my father, but he wasn't at home. I decided to wait until he returned and tell him, but before he came a friend telephoned me the news that Mion had killed himself, so I decided not to tell anyone, not even my father, that I had been in the studio, but to say that I had rung the bell and knocked on the door and got no reply. I thought that would make no difference, but it has now been explained to me that it does, and therefore I am stating it exactly as it happened.

As she got to the end the waiter came with the drinks, and she held the document against her chest as if it were a poker hand. Keeping it there with her left, she reached for the glass with her right and took a big swallow of scotch. I took a sip of mine to be sociable.

"It's a pack of lies," she said indignantly.

"It sure is," I agreed. "I have good ears, so keep your voice down. Mr. Wolfe is perfectly willing to give you a break, and anyhow it would be a job to get you to sign it if it told the truth. We are quite aware that the studio door was locked and you opened it with your key. Also that—no, listen to me a minute—also that you purposely picked up the gun and put it on the bust because you thought Mrs. Mion had killed him and left the gun there so it would look like suicide, and you wanted to mess it up for her. You couldn't—"

"Where were you?" she demanded scornfully. "Hiding behind the couch?"

"Nuts. If you didn't have a key why did you break a date to see me because of what I said on the phone? As for the gun, you couldn't have been dumber if you'd worked at it for a year. Who would believe anyone had shot him so it would look like suicide and then been fool enough to put the gun on the bust? Too dumb to believe, honest, but you did it."

She was too busy with her brain to resent being called dumb. Her frown creased her smooth pale forehead and took the glisten from her eyes. "Anyway," she protested, "what this says not only isn't true, it's impossible! They found the gun on the floor by his body, so this couldn't possibly be true!"

"Yeah." I grinned at her. "It must have been a shock when you read that in the paper. Since you had personally moved the gun to the bust, how come they found it on the floor? Obviously someone had moved it back. I suppose you decided that Mrs. Mion had done that too, and it must have been hard to keep your mouth shut, but you had to. Now it's different. Mr. Wolfe knows who put the gun back on the floor and he can prove it. What's more, he knows Mion was murdered and he can prove that too. All that stops him is the detail of explaining how the gun got from the floor to the bust." I got out my fountain pen. "Put your name to that, and I'll witness it, and we're all set."

"You mean sign this thing?" She was contemptuous. "I'm not *that* dumb."

I caught the waiter's eye and signaled for refills, and then, to keep her company, emptied my glass.

I met her gaze, matching her frown. "Lookit, Blue Eyes," I told her reasonably. "I'm not sticking needles under your nails. I'm not saying we can prove you entered the studio—whether with your key or because the door wasn't locked doesn't matter—and moved the gun. We know you did, since no one else could have and you were there at the right time, but I admit we can't prove it. However, I'm offering you a wonderful bargain."

I pointed the pen at her. "Just listen. All we want this statement for is to keep it in reserve, in case the person who put the gun back on the floor is fool enough to blab it, which is very unlikely. He would only be—"

"You say he?" she demanded.

"Make it he or she. As Mr. Wolfe says, the language could use another pronoun. He would only be making trouble for himself. If he doesn't spill it, and he won't, your statement won't be used at all, but we've got to have it in the safe in case he does. Another thing, if we have this statement we won't feel obliged to pass it along to the cops about your having had a key to the studio door. We wouldn't be interested in keys. Still another, you'll be saving your father a big chunk of dough. If you sign this statement we can clear up the matter of Mion's death, and if we do that I guarantee Mrs. Mion will be in no frame of mind to push any claim against your father. She will be too busy with a certain matter."

I proffered the pen. "Go ahead and sign it."

She shook her head, but not with much energy because her brain was working again. Fully appreciating the fact that her thinking was not on the tournament level, I was patient. Then the refills came and there was a recess, since she couldn't be expected to think and drink all at once. But finally she fought her way through to the point I had aimed at.

"So you know," she declared with satisfaction.

"We know enough," I said darkly.

"You know she killed him. You know she put the gun back on the floor. I knew that too, I knew she must have. And now you can prove it? If I sign this you can prove it?"

Of course I could have covered it with doubletalk, but I thought, What the hell. "We certainly can," I assured her. "With this statement we're ready to go. It's the missing link. Here's the pen."

She lifted her glass, drained it, put it down, and damned if she didn't shake her head again, this time with energy. "No," she said flatly, "I won't." She extended a hand with the document in it. "I admit it's all true, and when you get her on trial if she says she put the gun back on the floor I'll come and swear to it that I put it on the bust, but I won't sign anything because once I signed something about an accident and my father made me promise that I would never sign anything again without showing it to him first. I could take it and show it to him and then sign it, and you could come for it tonight or tomorrow." She frowned. "Except that he knows I had a key, but I could explain that."

But she no longer had the document. I had reached and taken it. You are welcome to think I should have changed holds on her and gone on fighting, but you weren't there seeing and hearing her, and I was. I gave up. I got out my pocket notebook, tore out a page, and began writing on it.

"I could use another drink," she stated.

"In a minute," I mumbled, and went on writing, as follows:

To Nero Wolfe:

I hereby declare that Archie Goodwin has tried his best to persuade me to sign the statement you wrote, and explained its purpose to me, and I have told him why I must refuse to sign it.

"There," I said, handing it to her. "That won't be signing something; it's just stating that you refuse to sign something. The reason I've got to have it, Mr. Wolfe knows how beautiful girls appeal to me, especially sophisticated girls like you, and if I take that thing back to him unsigned he'll think I didn't even try. He might even fire me. Just write your name there at the bottom."

She read it over again and took the pen. She smiled at me, glistening. "You're not kidding me any," she said, not unfriendly. "I know when I appeal to a man. You think I'm cold and calculating."

"Yeah?" I made it a little bitter, but not too bitter. "Anyhow it's not the point whether you appeal to me, but what Mr. Wolfe will think. It'll help a lot to have that. Much obliged." I took the paper from her and blew on her signature to dry it.

"I know when I appeal to a man," she stated.

There wasn't another thing there I wanted, but I had practically promised to buy her another drink, so I did so.

It was after six when I got back to West Thirty-fifth Street, so Wolfe had finished in the plant rooms and was down in the office. I marched in and put the unsigned statement on his desk in front of him.

He grunted. "Well?"

I sat down and told him exactly how it had gone, up to the point where she had offered to take the document home and show it to her father.

"I'm sorry," I said, "but some of her outstanding qualities didn't show much in that crowd the other evening. I give this not as an excuse but merely a fact. Her mental operations could easily be carried on inside a hollowed-out pea. Knowing what you think of unsupported statements, and wanting to convince you of the truth of that one. I got evidence to back it up. Here's a paper she *did* sign."

I handed him the page I had torn from my notebook. He took a look at it and then cocked an eye at me.

"She signed this?"

"Yes, sir. In my presence."

"Indeed. Good. Satisfactory."

I acknowledged the tribute with a careless nod. It does not hurt my feelings when he says, "Satisfactory," like that.

"A bold, easy hand," he said. "She used your pen?"

"Yes, sir."

"May I have it, please?"

I arose and handed it to him, together with a couple of sheets of typewriter paper, and stood and watched with interested approval as he wrote "Clara James" over and over again, comparing each attempt with the sample I had secured. Meanwhile, at intervals, he spoke.

"It's highly unlikely that anyone will ever see it— except our clients. . . . That's better. . . . There's time to phone all of them before dinner—first Mrs. Mion and Mr. Weppler—then the others. . . . Tell them my opinion is ready on Mrs. Mion's claim against Mr. James. . . . If they can come at nine this evening —If that's impossible tomorrow morning at eleven will do. . . . Then get Mr. Cramer. . . . Tell him it might be well to bring one of his men along. . . ."

He flattened the typed statement on his desk blotter, forged Clara James' name at the bottom, and compared it with the true signature which I had provided.

"Faulty, to an expert," he muttered, "but no expert will ever see it. For our clients, even if they know her writing, it will do nicely."

VIII

It took a solid hour on the phone to get it fixed for that evening, but I finally managed it. I never did catch up with Gifford James, but his daughter agreed to find him and deliver him, and made good on it. The others I tracked down myself.

The only ones that gave me an argument were the clients, especially Peggy Mion. She balked hard at sitting in at a meeting for the ostensible purpose of collecting from Gifford James, and I had to appeal to Wolfe. Fred and Peggy were invited to come ahead of the others for a private briefing and then decide whether to stay or not. She bought that.

They got there in time to help out with the after-dinner coffee. Peggy had presumably brushed her teeth and had a nap and a bath, and manifestly she had changed her clothes, but even so she did not sparkle. She was wary, weary, removed, and skeptical. She didn't say in so many words that she wished she had never gone near Nero Wolfe, but she might as well have. I had a notion that Fred Weppler felt the same way about it but was being gallant and loyal. It was Peggy who had insisted on coming to Wolfe, and Fred didn't want her to feel that he thought she had made things worse instead of better.

They didn't perk up even when Wolfe showed them the statement with Clara James' name signed to it. They read it together, with her in the red leather chair and him perched on the arm.

They looked up together, at Wolfe.

"So what?" Fred demanded.

"My dear sir." Wolfe pushed his cup and saucer back. "My dear madam. Why did you come to me? Because the fact that the gun was not on the floor when you two entered the studio convinced you that Mion had not killed himself but had been murdered. If the circumstances had permitted you to believe that he had killed himself, you would be married by now and never have needed me. Very well. That is now precisely what the circumstances are. What more do you want? You wanted your minds cleared. I have cleared them."

Fred twisted his lips, tight.

"I don't believe it," Peggy said glumly.

"You don't believe this statement?" Wolfe reached for the document and put it in his desk drawer, which struck me as a wise precaution, since it was getting close to nine o'clock. "Do you think Miss James would sign a thing like that if it weren't true? Why would—"

"I don't mean that," Peggy said. "I mean I don't believe my husband killed himself, no matter where the gun was. I knew him too well. He would never have killed himself—*never*." She twisted her head to look up at her fellow client. "Would he, Fred?"

"It's hard to believe," Fred admitted grudgingly.

"I see." Wolfe was caustic. "Then the job you hired me for was not as you described it. At least, you must concede that I have satisfied you about the gun; you can't wiggle out of that. So that job's done, but now you want more. You want a murder disclosed, which means, of necessity, a murderer caught. You want—"

"I only mean," Peggy insisted forlornly, "that I don't believe he killed himself, and nothing would make me believe it. I see now what I really—"

The doorbell sounded, and I went to answer it.

IX

So the clients stayed for the party.

There were ten guests altogether: the six who had been there Monday evening, the two clients, Inspector Cramer, and my old friend and enemy, Sergeant Purley Stebbins. What made it unusual was that the dumbest one of the lot, Clara James, was the only one who had a notion of what was up, unless she had told her father, which I doubted. She had the advantage of the lead I had given her at the Churchill bar. Adele Bosley, Dr. Lloyd, Rupert Grove, Judge Arnold, and Gifford James had had no reason to suppose there was anything on the agenda but the damage claim against James, until they got there and were made acquainted with Inspector Cramer and Sergeant Stebbins. God only knew what they thought then; one glance at their faces was enough to show *they* didn't know. As for Cramer and Stebbins, they had had enough experience of Nero Wolfe to be aware that almost certainly fur was going to fly, but whose and how and when? And as for Fred and Peggy, even after the arrival of the law, they probably thought that Wolfe was going to get Mion's suicide pegged down by producing Clara's statement and disclosing what Fred had told us about moving the gun from the bust to the floor, which accounted for the desperate and cornered look on their faces. But now they were stuck.

Wolfe focused on the inspector, who was seated in the rear over by the big globe, with Purley nearby. "If you don't mind, Mr. Cramer, first I'll clear up a little matter that is outside your interest."

Cramer nodded and shifted the cigar in his mouth to a new angle. He was keeping his watchful eyes on the move.

Wolfe changed his focus. "I'm sure you'll all be glad to hear this. Not that I formed my opinion so as to please you; I considered only the merits of the case. Without prejudice to her legal position, I feel that morally Mrs. Mion has no claim on Mr. James. As I said she would, she accepts my judgment. She makes no claim and will ask no payment for damages. You verify that before these witnesses, Mrs. Mion?"

"Certainly." Peggy was going to add something, but stopped it on the way out.

"This is wonderful!" Adele Bosley was out of her chair. "May I use a phone?"

"Later," Wolfe snapped at her. "Sit down, please."

"It seems to me," Judge Arnold observed, "that this could have been told us on the phone. I had to cancel an important engagement." Lawyers are never satisfied.

"Quite true," Wolfe agreed mildly, "if that were all. But there's the matter of Mion's death. When I—"

"What has that got to do with it?"

"I'm about to tell you. Surely it isn't extraneous, since his death resulted, though indirectly, from the assault by Mr. James. But my interest goes beyond that. Mrs. Mion hired me not only to decide about the claim of her husband's estate against Mr. James—that is now closed—but also to investigate her husband's death. She was convinced he had not killed himself. She could not believe it was in his character to commit suicide. I have investigated and I am prepared to report to her."

"You don't need us here for that," Rupert the Fat said in a high squeak.

"I need one of you. I need the murderer."

"You still don't need *us*," Arnold said harshly.

"Hang it," Wolfe snapped, "then go! All but one of you. Go!"

Nobody made a move.

Wolfe gave them five seconds. "Then I'll go on," he said dryly. "As I say, I'm prepared to report, but the investigation is not concluded. One vital detail will require official sanction, and that's why Inspector Cramer is present. It will also need Mrs. Mion's concurrence; and I think it well to consult Dr. Lloyd too, since he signed the death certificate." His eyes went to Peggy. "First you, madam. Will you give your consent to the exhumation of your husband's body?"

She gawked at him. "What for?"

"To get evidence that he was murdered, and by whom. It is a reasonable expectation."

She stopped gawking. "Yes. I don't care." She thought he was just talking to hear himself.

Wolfe's eyes went left. "You have no objection, Dr. Lloyd?" Lloyd was nonplused. "I have no idea," he said slowly and distinctly, "what you're getting at, but in any case I have no voice in the matter. I merely issued the certificate."

"Then you won't oppose it. Mr. Cramer. The basis for the request for official sanction will appear in a moment, but you should know that what will be required is an examination and report by Dr. Abraham Rentner of Mount Sinai Hospital."

"You don't get an exhumation just because you're curious," Cramer growled.

"I know it. I'm more than curious." Wolfe's eyes traveled. "You all know, I suppose, that one of the chief reasons, probably the main one, for the police decision that Mion had committed suicide was the manner of his death. Of course other details had to fit—as for instance the presence of the gun there beside the body—

and they did. But the determining factor was the assumption that a man cannot be murdered by sticking the barrel of a revolver in his mouth and pulling the trigger unless he is first made unconscious; and there was no evidence that Mion had been either struck or drugged, and besides, when the bullet left his head it went to the ceiling. However, though that assumption is ordinarily sound, surely this case was an exception. It came to my mind at once, when Mrs. Mion first consulted me. For there was present— But I'll show you with a simple demonstration. Archie. Get a gun."

I opened my third drawer and got one out.

"Is it loaded?"

I flipped it open to check. "No, sir."

Wolfe returned to the audience. "You, I think, Mr. James. As an opera singer you should be able to follow stage directions. Stand up, please. This is a serious matter, so do it right. You are a patient with a sore throat, and Mr. Goodwin is your doctor. He will ask you to open your mouth so he can look at your throat. You are to do exactly what you would naturally do under those circumstances. Will you do that?"

"But it's obvious." James, standing, was looking grim. "I don't need to."

"Nevertheless, please indulge me. There's a certain detail. Will you do it as naturally as possible?"

"Yes."

"Good. Will the rest of you all watch Mr. James' face? Closely. Go ahead, Archie."

With the gun in my pocket I moved in front of James and told him to open wide. He did so. For a moment his eyes came to mine as I peered into his throat, and then slanted upward. Not in a hurry, I took the gun from my pocket and poked it into his mouth until it touched the roof. He jerked back and dropped into his chair.

"Did you see the gun?" Wolfe demanded.

"No. My eyes were up."

"Just so." Wolfe looked at the others. "You saw his eyes go up? They always do. Try it yourselves sometime. I tried it in my bedroom Sunday evening. So it is by no means impossible to kill a man that way, it isn't even difficult, if you're a doctor and he has something wrong with his throat. You agree, Dr. Lloyd?"

Lloyd had not joined the general movement to watch James' face during the demonstration. He hadn't stirred a muscle. Now his jaw was twitching a little, but that was all.

He did his best to smile. "To show that a thing could happen," he said in a pretty good voice, "isn't the same thing as proving it did happen."

"Indeed it isn't," Wolfe conceded. "Though we do have some facts. You have no effective alibi. Mion would have admitted you to his studio at any time without question. You could have managed easily to get the gun from the base of Caruso's bust, and slipped it into your pocket without being seen. For you, as for no one else, he would upon request have stood with his mouth wide open, inviting his doom. He was killed shortly after you had been compelled to make an appointment for Dr. Rentner to examine him. We do have those facts, don't we?"

"They prove nothing," Lloyd insisted. His voice was not quite as good. He came out of his chair to his feet. It did not look as if the movement had any purpose; apparently he simply couldn't stay put in his chair, and the muscles had acted on their own. And it had been a mistake because, standing upright, he began to tremble.

"They'll help," Wolfe told him, "if we can get one more—and I suspect we can, or what are you quivering about? What was it, Doctor? Some unfortunate blunder? Had you botched the operation and ruined his voice forever? I suppose that was it, since the threat to your reputation and career was grave enough to make you resort to murder. Anyhow we'll soon know, when Dr. Rentner makes his examination and reports. I don't expect you to furnish—"

"It wasn't a blunder!" Lloyd squawked. "It could have happened to anyone—"

Whereupon he did blunder. I think what made him lose his head completely was hearing his own voice and realizing it was a hysterical squawk and he couldn't help it. He made a dash for the door. I knocked Judge Arnold down in my rush across the room, which was unnecessary, for by the time I arrived Purley Stebbins had Lloyd by the collar, and Cramer was there too. Hearing a commotion behind me, I turned around. Clara James had made a dive for Peggy Mion, screeching something I didn't catch, but her father and Adele Bosley had stopped her and were getting her under control. Judge Arnold and Rupert the Fat were excitedly telling Wolfe how wonderful he was. Peggy was apparently weeping, from the way her shoulders were shaking, but I couldn't see her face because it was buried on Fred's shoulder, and his arms had her tight.

Nobody wanted me or needed me, so I went to the kitchen for a glass of milk.

**Bullet
for One**

I

It was her complexion that made it hard to believe she was as scared as she said she was.

"Maybe I haven't made it clear," she persisted, twisting her fingers some more though I had asked her to stop. "I'm not making anything up, really I'm not. If they framed me once, isn't that a good enough reason to think they are doing it again?"

If her cheek color had been from a drugstore, with the patches showing because the fear in her heart was using extra blood for internal needs, I would probably have been affected more. But at first sight of her I had been reminded of a picture on a calendar hanging on the wall of Sam's Diner on Eleventh Avenue, a picture of a round-faced girl with one hand holding a pail and the other hand resting on the flank of a cow she had just milked or was going to milk. It was her to a T, in skin tint, build, and innocence.

She quit the finger-twisting to make tight little fists and perch them on her thigh fronts. "Is he really such a puffed-up baboon?" she demanded. "They'll be here in twenty minutes, and I've got to see him first!"

Suddenly she was out of the chair, on her feet. "Where is he, upstairs?"

Having suspected she was subject to impulses, I had, instead of crossing to my desk, held a position between her and the door to the hall.

"Give it up," I advised her. "When you stand up you tremble, I noticed that when you came in, so sit down. I've tried to explain, Miss Rooney, that while this room is Mr. Wolfe's office, the rest of this building is his home. From nine to eleven in the morning, and from four to six in the afternoon, he is absolutely at home, up in the plant rooms with his orchids, and bigger men than you have had to like it. But, what I've seen of you, I think possibly you're nice, and I'll do you a favor."

"What?"

"Sit down and quit trembling."

She sat down.

"I'll go up and tell him about you."

"What will you tell him?"

"I'll remind him that a man named Ferdinand Pohl phoned this morning and made a date for himself and four others, to come here to see Mr. Wolfe at six o'clock, which is sixteen minutes from now. I'll tell him your name is Audrey Rooney and you're one of the four others, and you're fairly good-looking and may be nice, and you're scared stiff because, as you tell it, they're pretending they think it was Talbott but actually they're getting set to frame you, and—"

"Not all of them."

"Anyhow some. I'll tell him that you came ahead of time to see him alone and inform him that you have not murdered anyone, specifically not Sigmund Keyes, and to warn him that he must watch these stinkers like a hawk."

"It sounds crazy—like that!"

"I'll put feeling in it."

She left her chair again, came to me in three swift steps, flattened her palms on my coat front, and tilted her head back to get my eyes.

"You may be nice too," she said hopefully.

"That would be too much to expect," I told her as I turned and made for the stairs in the hall.

II

Ferdinand Pohl was speaking.

Sitting there in the office with my chair swiveled so that my back was to my desk, with Wolfe himself behind his desk to my left, I took Pohl in. He was close to twice my age. Seated in the red leather chair beyond the end of Wolfe's desk, with his leg-crossing histing his pants so that five inches of bare shin showed above his garterless sock, there was nothing about him to command attention except an unusual assortment of facial creases, and nothing at all to love.

"What brought us together," he was saying in a thin peevish tone, "and what brought us here together, is our unanimous opinion that Sigmund Keyes was murdered by Victor Talbott, and also our conviction—"

"Not unanimous," another voice objected.

The voice was soft and good for the ears, and its owner was good for the eyes. Her chin, especially, was the kind you can take from any angle. The only reason I hadn't seated her in the chair nearest mine was that on her arrival she had answered my welcoming smile with nothing but brow-lifting, and I had decided to hell with her until she learned her manners.

"Not unanimous, Ferdy," she objected.

"You said," Pohl told her, even more peevish, "that you were in sympathy with our purpose and wanted to join us and come here with us."

Seeing them and hearing them, I made a note that they hated each other. She had known him longer than I had, since she called him Ferdy, and evidently she agreed that there was nothing about him to love. I was about to start feeling that I had been too harsh with her when I saw she was lifting her brows at him.

"That," she declared, "is quite different from having the opinion that Vic murdered my father. I have no opinion, because I don't know."

"Then what are you in sympathy with?"

"I want to find out. So do you. And I certainly agree that the police are being extremely stupid."

"Who do you think killed him if Vic didn't?"

"I don't know." The brows went up again. "But since I have inherited my father's business, and since I am engaged to marry Vic, and since a few other things, I want very much to know. That's why I'm here with you."

"You don't belong here!"

"I'm here, Ferdy."

"I say you don't belong!" Pohl's creases were wriggling. "I said so and I still say so! We came, the four of us, for a definite purpose, to get Nero Wolfe to find proof that Vic killed your father!" Pohl suddenly uncrossed his legs, leaned forward to peer at Dorothy Keyes' face, and asked in a mean little voice, "And what if you helped him?"

Three other voices spoke at once. One said, "They're off again."

Another, "Let Mr. Broadyke tell it."

Another, "Get one of them out of here."

Wolfe said, "If the job is limited to those terms, Mr.

Pohl, to prove that a man named by you committed murder, you've wasted your trip. What if he didn't?"

III

Many things had happened in that office on the ground floor of the old brownstone house owned by Nero Wolfe during the years I had worked for him as his man Friday, Saturday, Sunday, Monday, Tuesday, Wednesday, and Thursday.

This gathering in the office, on this Tuesday evening in October, had its own special angle of interest. Sigmund Keyes, top-drawer industrial designer, had been murdered the preceding Tuesday, just a week ago. I had read about it in the papers and had also found an opportunity to hear it privately discussed by my friend and enemy Sergeant Purley Stebbins of Homicide, and from the professional-detective slant it struck me as a lulu.

It had been Keyes' custom, five days a week at six-thirty in the morning, to take a walk in the park, and to do it the hard and silly way by walking on four legs instead of two. He kept the four legs, which he owned and which were named Casanova, at the Stillwell Riding Academy on Ninety-eighth Street just west of the park. That morning he mounted Casanova as usual, promptly at six-thirty, and rode into the park. Forty minutes later, at seven-ten, he had been seen by a mounted cop, in the park on patrol, down around Sixty-sixth Street. His customary schedule would have had him about there at that time. Twenty-five minutes later, at seven-thirty-five, Casanova, with his saddle uninhabited, had emerged from the park uptown and strolled down the street to the academy. Curiosity had naturally been aroused, and in three-quarters of an hour had been satisfied, when a park cop had found Keyes' body behind a thicket some twenty yards from the bridle path in the park, in the latitude of Ninety-fifth Street. Later a .38-caliber revolver bullet had been dug out of his chest. The police had concluded, from marks on the path and beyond its edge, that he had been shot out of his saddle and had crawled, with difficulty, up a little slope toward a paved walk for pedestrians, and hadn't had enough life left to make it.

A horseman shot from his saddle within sight of the Empire State Building was of course a natural for the tabloids, and the other papers thought well of it too. No weapon had been found, and no eyewitnesses. No citizen had even come forward to report seeing a masked man lurking behind a tree, probably because very few New Yorkers could possibly explain being up and dressed and strolling in the park at that hour of the morning.

So the city employees had had to start at the other end and look for motives and opportunities. During the week that had passed a lot of names had been mentioned and a lot of people had received official callers, and as a result the glare had pretty well concentrated on six spots. So the papers had it, and so I gathered from Purley Stebbins. What gave the scene in our office that Tuesday afternoon its special angle of interest was the fact that five of the six spots were there seated on chairs, and apparently what they wanted Wolfe to do was to take the glare out of their eyes and get it aimed exclusively at the sixth spot, not present.

IV

"Permit me to say," Frank Broadyke offered in a cultivated baritone, "that Mr. Pohl has put it badly. The situation is this, Mr. Wolfe, that Mr. Pohl got us together and we found that each of us feels that he is being harassed unreasonably. Not only that he is unjustly suspected of a crime he did not commit, but that in a full week the police have accomplished nothing and aren't likely to, and we will be left with this unjust suspicion permanently upon us."

Broadyke gestured with a hand. More than his baritone was cultivated; he was cultivated all over. He was somewhat younger than Pohl, and ten times as elegant. His manner gave the impression that he was finding it difficult just to be himself because (a) he was in the office of a private detective, which was vulgar, (b) he had come there with persons with whom one doesn't ordinarily associate, which was embarrassing, and (c) the subject for discussion was his connection with a murder, which was preposterous.

He was going on. "Mr. Pohl suggested that we consult you and engage your services. As one who will gladly pay my share of the bill, permit me to say that what I want is the removal of that unjust suspicion. If you can achieve that only by finding the criminal and evidence against him, very well. If the guilty man proves to be Victor Talbott, again very well."

"There's no if about it!" Pohl blurted. "Talbott did it, and the job is to pin it on him!"

"With me helping, Ferdy, don't forget," Dorothy Keyes told him softly.

"Aw, can it!"

Eyes turned to the speaker, whose only contribution up to that point had been the remark, "They're off again." Heads had to turn too because he was seated to the rear of the swing of the arc. The high pitch of his voice was a good match for his name, Wayne Safford, but not for his broad husky build and the strong big bones of his face. According to the papers he was twenty-eight, but he looked a little older, about my age.

Wolfe nodded at him. "I quite agree, Mr. Safford." Wolfe's eyes swept the arc. "Mr. Pohl wants too much for his money. You can hire me to catch a fish, ladies and gentlemen, but you can't tell me which fish. You can tell me what it is I'm after—a murderer—but you can't tell me who it is unless you have evidence, and in that case why pay me? Have you got evidence?"

No one said anything.

"Have you got evidence, Mr. Pohl?"

"No."

"How do you know it was Mr. Talbott?"

"I know it, that's all. We all know it! Even Miss Keyes here knows it, but she's too damn contrary to admit it."

Wolfe swept the arc again. "Is that true? Do you all know it?"

No word. No "yes" and no "no." No nods and no shakes.

"Then the identity of the fish is left to me. Is that understood? Mr. Broadyke?"

"Yes."

"Mr. Safford?"

"Yes."

"Miss Rooney?"

"Yes. Only I think it was Vic Talbott."

"Nothing can stop you. Miss Keyes?"

"Yes."

"Mr. Pohl?"

No answer.

"I must have a commitment on this, Mr. Pohl. If it proves to be Mr. Talbott you can pay extra. But in any case, I am hired to get facts?"

"Sure, the real facts."

"There is no other kind. I guarantee not to deliver any unreal facts." Wolfe leaned forward to press a button on his desk. "That is, indeed, the only guaranty I can give you. I should make it plain that you are responsible both collectively and individually for this engagement with me. Now if—"

The door to the hall had opened, and Fritz Brenner entered and approached.

"Fritz," Wolfe told him, "there will be five guests at dinner."

"Yes, sir," Fritz told him without a blink and turned to go. That's how good Fritz is, and he is not the kind to ring in omelets or canned soup. As he was opening the door a protest came from Frank Broadyke.

"Better make it four. I'll have to leave soon and I have a dinner engagement."

"Cancel it," Wolfe snapped.

"I'm afraid I can't, really."

"Then I can't take this job." Wolfe was curt. "What do you expect, with this thing already a week old?" He glanced at the clock on the wall. "I'll need you, all of you, certainly all evening, and probably most of the night. I must know all that you know about Mr. Keyes and Mr. Talbott. Also, if I am to remove this unjust suspicion of you from the minds of the police and the public, I must begin by removing it from my own mind. That will take many hours of hard work."

"Oh," Dorothy Keyes put in, her brows going up, "you suspect us, do you?"

Wolfe, ignoring her, asked Broadyke, "Well, sir?"

"I'll have to phone," Broadyke muttered.

"You may," Wolfe conceded, as if he were yielding a point. His eyes moved, left and right and left again, and settled on Audrey Rooney, whose chair was a little in the rear, to one side of Wayne Safford's. "Miss Rooney," he shot at her, "you seem to be the most vulnerable, since you were on the scene. When did Mr. Keyes dismiss you from his employ, and what for?"

Audrey had been sitting straight and still, with her lips tight. "Well, it was—" she began, but stopped to clear her throat and then didn't continue because of an interruption.

The doorbell had rung, and I had left it to Fritz to answer it, which was the custom when I was engaged with Wolfe and visitors, unless superseding orders had been given. Now the door to the hall opened, and Fritz entered, closed the door behind him, and announced. "A gentleman to see you, sir. Mr. Victor Talbott."

The name plopped in the middle of us like a paratrooper at a picnic.

"By God!" Wayne Safford exclaimed.

"How the devil—" Frank Broadyke started, and stopped.

"So you told him!" Pohl spat at Dorothy Keyes.

Dorothy merely raised her brows. I was getting fed up with that routine and wished she would try something else.

Audrey Rooney's mouth was hanging open.

"Show him in," Wolfe told Fritz.

V

Like millions of my fellow citizens, I had done some sizing up of Victor Talbott from pictures of him in the papers, and within ten seconds after he had joined us in the office I had decided the label I had tied on him could stay. He was the guy who, at a cocktail party or before dinner, grabs the tray of appetizers and passes it around, looking into eyes and making cracks.

Not counting me, he was easily the best-looking male in the room.

Entering, he shot a glance and a smile at Dorothy Keyes, ignored the others, came to a stop in front of Wolfe's desk, and said pleasantly, "You're Nero Wolfe, of course. I'm Vic Talbott. I suppose you'd rather not shake hands with me under the circumstances—that is, if you're accepting the job these people came to offer you. Are you?"

"How do you do, sir," Wolfe rumbled. "Good heavens, I've shaken hands with—how many murderers, Archie?"

"Oh—forty," I estimated.

"At least that. That's Mr. Goodwin, Mr. Talbott."

Evidently Vic figured I might be squeamish too, for he gave me a nod but extended no hand. Then he turned to face the guests. "What about it, folks? Have you hired the great detective?"

"Nuts," Wayne Safford squeaked at him. "You come prancing in, huh?"

Ferdinand Pohl had left his chair and was advancing on the gate-crasher. I was on my feet, ready to move. There was plenty of feeling loose in the room, and I didn't want any of our clients hurt. But all Pohl did was to tap Talbott on the chest with a thick forefinger and growl at him, "Listen, my boy. You're not going to sell anything here. You've made one sale too many as it is." Pohl whirled to Wolfe. "What did you let him in for?"

"Permit me to say," Broadyke put in, "that it does seem an excess of hospitality."

"By the way, Vic"—it was Dorothy's soft voice—"Ferdy says I was your accomplice."

The remarks from the others had made no visible impression on him, but it was different with Dorothy. He turned to her, and the look on his face was good for a whole chapter in his biography. He was absolutely all hers unless I needed an oculist. She could lift her lovely brows a thousand times a day without feeding him up. He let his eyes speak to her and then wheeled to use his tongue for Pohl. "Do you know what I think of you, Ferdy? I guess you do!"

"If you please," Wolfe said sharply. "You don't need my office for exchanging your opinions of one another; you can do that anywhere. We have work to do. Mr. Talbott, you asked if I've accepted a job that has been offered me. I have. I have engaged to investigate the murder of Sigmund Keyes. But I have received no confidences and can still decline it. Have you a better offer? What did you come here for?"

Talbott smiled at him. "That's the way to talk," he said admiringly. "No, I have nothing to offer in the way of a job, but I felt I ought to be in on this. I figured it this way: they were going to hire you to get me arrested for murder, so naturally you would like to have a look at me and ask me some questions—and here I am."

"Pleading not guilty, of course. Archie. A chair for Mr. Talbott."

"Of course," he agreed, thanking me with a smile for the chair I brought, and sitting down. "Otherwise you'd have no job. Shoot." Suddenly he flushed. "Under the circumstances, I guess I shouldn't have said 'shoot.'"

"You could have said 'Fire away,'" Wayne Safford piped up from the rear.

"Be quiet, Wayne," Audrey Rooney scolded him.

"Permit me—" Broadyke began, but Wolfe cut him off.

"No. Mr. Talbott has invited questions." He focused on the inviter. "These other people think the police are handling this matter stupidly and ineffectively. Do you agree, Mr. Talbott?"

Vic considered a moment, then nodded. "On the whole, yes," he assented.

"Why?"

"Well—you see, they're up against it. They're used to working with clues, and while they found plenty of clues to show what happened, like the marks on the bridle path and leading to the thicket, there aren't any that help to identify the murderer. Absolutely none whatever. So they had to fall back on motive, and right away they found a man with the best motive in the world."

Talbott tapped himself on the necktie. "Me. But then they found that his man—me—that I couldn't possibly have done it because I was somewhere else. They found I had an alibi that was—"

"Phony!" From Wayne Safford.

"Made to order." From Broadyke.

"The dumbheads!" From Pohl. "If they had brains enough to give that switchboard girl—"

"Please!" Wolfe shut them up. "Go ahead, Mr. Talbott. Your alibi—but first the motive. What is the best motive in the world?"

Vic looked surprised. "It's been printed over and over again."

"I know. But I don't want journalistic conjectures when I've got you—unless you're sensitive about it."

Talbott's smile had some bitterness in it. "If I was," he declared, "I've sure been cured this past week. I guess ten million people have read that I'm deeply in love with Dorothy Keyes or some variation of that. All right, I am! Want a shot—want a picture of me saying it?" He turned to face his fiancée. "I love you, Dorothy, better than all the world, deeply, madly, with all my heart." He returned to Wolfe. "There's your motive."

"Vic, darling," Dorothy told his profile, "you're a perfect fool, and you're perfectly fascinating. I really am glad you've got a good alibi."

"You demonstrate love," Wolfe said dryly, "by killing your beloved's surviving parent. Is that it?"

"Yes," Talbott asserted. "Under certain conditions. Here was the situation. Sigmund Keyes was the most celebrated and successful industrial designer in America, and—"

"Nonsense!" Broadyke exploded, without asking permission to say.

Talbott smiled. "Sometimes," he said, as if offering it for consideration, "a jealous man is worse than any jealous woman. You know, of course, that Mr. Broadyke is himself an industrial designer—in fact, he practically invented the profession. Not many manufacturers would dream of tooling for a new model —steamship, railroad train, airplane, refrigerator, vacuum cleaner, alarm clock, no matter what—without consulting Broadyke, until I came along and took over the selling end for Sigmund Keyes. Incidentally, that's why I doubt if Broadyke killed Keyes. If he had got that desperate about it he wouldn't have killed Keyes, he would have killed me."

"You were speaking," Wolfe reminded him, "of love as a motive for murder under certain conditions."

"Yes, and Broadyke threw me off." Talbott cocked his head. "Let's see—oh, yes, and I was doing the selling for Keyes, and he couldn't stand the talk going around that I was mostly responsible for the big success we were having, but he was afraid to get rid of me. And I loved his daughter and wanted her to marry me, and will always love her. But he had great influence with her, which I did not and do not understand— anyway, if she loved me as I do her that wouldn't have mattered, but she doesn't—"

"My God, Vic," Dorothy protested, "haven't I said a dozen times I'd marry you like that"—she snapped her fingers—"if it weren't for Dad? Really, I'm crazy about you!"

"All right," Talbott told Wolfe, "there's your motive. It's certainly old-fashioned, no modern industrial design to it, but it's absolutely dependable. Naturally that's what the police thought until they ran up against the fact that I was somewhere else. That got them bewildered and made them sore, and they haven't recovered their wits, so I guess my good friends here are right that they're being stupid and ineffective. Not that they've crossed me off entirely. I understand they've got an army of detectives and stool pigeons hunting for the gunman I hired to do the job. They'll have to hunt hard. You heard Miss Keyes call me a fool, but I'm not quite fool enough to hire someone to commit a murder for me."

"I should hope not." Wolfe sighed. "There's nothing better than a good motive. What about the alibi? Have the police given up on that?"

"Yes, the damn idiots!" Pohl blurted. "That switch-board girl—"

"I asked Mr. Talbott," Wolfe snapped.

"I don't know," Talbott admitted, "but I suppose they had to. I'm still trembling at how lucky I was that I got to bed late that Monday night—I mean a week ago, the night before Keyes was killed. If I had been riding with him I'd be in jail now, and done for. It's a question of timing."

Talbott compressed his lips and loosened them. "Oh, boy! The mounted cop saw Keyes riding in the park near Sixty-sixth Street at ten minutes past seven. Keyes was killed near Ninety-sixth Street. Even if he had galloped all the way he couldn't have got there, the way that bridle path winds, before seven-twenty. And he didn't gallop, because if he had the horse would have shown it, and he didn't." Talbott twisted around. "You're the authority on that, Wayne. Casanova hadn't been in a sweat, had he?"

"You're telling it," was all he got from Wayne Safford.

"Well, he hadn't," Talbott told Wolfe. "Wayne is on record on that. So Keyes couldn't have reached the spot where he was killed before seven-twenty-five. There's the time for that, twenty-five minutes past seven."

"And you?" Wolfe inquired.

"Me, I was lucky. I often rode in the park with Keyes at that ungodly hour—two or three times a week. He wanted me to make it every day, but I got out of it about half the time. There was nothing social or sociable about it. We would walk our horses side by side, talking business, except when he felt like trotting. I live at the Hotel Churchill. I got in late Monday night, but I left a call for six o'clock anyway, because I hadn't ridden with Keyes for several days and didn't want to get him sore. But when the girl rang my phone in the morning I was just too damn sleepy, and I told her to call the riding academy and say I wouldn't be there, and to call me again at seven-thirty. She did so, and I still didn't feel like turning out but I had to because I had a breakfast date with an out-of-town customer, so I told her to send up a double orange juice. A few minutes later a waiter brought it up. So was I lucky? Keyes was killed uptown at twenty-five past seven at the earliest, and probably a little later. I was in my room at the Churchill, nearly three miles away, at half-past seven. You can have three guesses how glad I was I left that seven-thirty call!"

Wolfe nodded. "You should give the out-of-town customer a discount. In that armor, why did you take the trouble to join this gathering?"

"A switchboard girl and a waiter, for God's sake!" Pohl snorted sarcastically.

"Nice honest people, Ferdy," Talbott told him, and answered Wolfe, "I didn't."

"No? You're not here?"

"Sure I'm here, but not to join any gathering. I came to join Miss Keyes. I don't regard it as trouble to join Miss Keyes. As for the rest of them, except maybe Broadyke—"

The doorbell rang again, and since additional gate-crashers might or might not be desirable, I upped myself in a hurry, stepped across and into the hall, intercepted Fritz just in time, and went to the front door to take a look through the panel of one-way glass.

Seeing who it was out on the stoop, I fastened the chain bolt, pulled the door open the two inches the chain would permit, and spoke through the crack. "I don't want to catch cold."

"Neither do I," a gruff voice told me. "Take that damn bolt off."

"Mr. Wolfe is engaged," I said politely. "Will I do?"

"You will not. You never have and you never will."

"Then hold it a minute. I'll see."

I shut the door, went to the office, and told Wolfe, "The man about the chair," which was my favorite alias for Inspector Cramer of Homicide.

Wolfe grunted and shook his head. "I'll be busy for hours and can't be interrupted."

I returned to the front, opened to the crack again, and said regretfully, "Sorry, but he's doing his homework."

"Yeah," Cramer said sarcastically, "he certainly is. Now that Talbott's here too you've got a full house. All six of 'em. Open the door."

"Bah. Who are you trying to impress? You have tails on one or more, possibly all, and I do hope you haven't abandoned Talbott because we like him. By the way, the phone girl and the waiter at the Churchill— what're their names?"

"I'm coming in, Goodwin."

"Come ahead. This chain has never had a real test, and I've wondered about it."

"In the name of the law, open this door!"

I was so astonished that I nearly did open it in order to get a good look at him. Through the crack I could use only one eye. "Well, listen to you," I said incredulously. "On me you try that? As you know, it's the law that keeps you out. If you're ready to make an arrest, tell me who, and I'll see that he or she doesn't pull a scoot. After all, you're not a monopoly. You've had them for a full week, day or night, and Wolfe has had them only an hour or so, and you can't bear it! Incidentally, they're not refusing to see you, they don't know you're here, so don't chalk that against them. It's Mr. Wolfe who can't be disturbed. I'll give you this much satisfaction: he hasn't solved it yet, and it may take till midnight. It will save time if you'll give me the names—"

"Shut up," Cramer rasped. "I came here perfectly friendly. There's no law against Wolfe having people in his office. And there's no law against my being there with them, either."

"There sure isn't," I agreed heartily, "once you're in, but what about this door? Here's a legal door, with a man on one side who can't open it, and a man on the other side who won't, and according to the statutes—"

"Archie!" It was a bellow from the office, Wolfe's loudest bellow, seldom heard, and there were other sounds. It came again. "Archie!"

I said hastily, "Excuse me," slammed the door shut, ran down the hall and turned the knob, and popped in.

It was nothing seriously alarming. Wolfe was still in his chair behind his desk. The chair Talbott had occupied was overturned. Dorothy was on her feet, her back to Wolfe's desk, with her brows elevated to a record high. Audrey Rooney was standing in the corner by the big globe, with her clenched fists pressed against her cheeks, staring. Pohl and Broadyke were also out of their chairs, also gazing at the center of the room. From the spectators' frozen attitudes you might have expected to see something really startling, but it was only a couple of guys slinging punches. As I entered Talbott landed a right hook on the side of Safford's neck, and as I closed the door to the hall behind me Safford countered with a solid stiff left to Talbott's kidney sector. The only noise besides their fists and feet was a tense mutter from Audrey Rooney in her corner. "Hit him, Wayne; hit him, Wayne."

"How much did I miss?" I demanded.

"Stop them!" Wolfe ordered me.

Talbott's right glanced off of Safford's cheek, and Safford got in another one over the kidney. They were operating properly and in an orderly manner, but Wolfe was the boss and he hated commotion in the office, so I stepped across, grabbed Talbott's coat collar and yanked him back so hard he fell over a chair, and faced Safford to block him. For a second I thought Safford was going to paste me with one he had waiting, but he let it drop.

"What started it so quick?" I wanted to know.

Audrey was there, clutching my sleeve, protesting fiercely, "You shouldn't have stopped him! Wayne could have knocked him down! He did before!" She sounded more bloodthirsty than milkthirsty.

"He made a remark about Miss Rooney," Broadyke permitted himself to say.

"Get him out of here!" Wolfe spluttered.

"Which one?" I asked, watching Safford with one eye and Talbott with the other.

"Mr. Talbott!"

"You did very well, Vic," Dorothy was saying. "You were fantastically handsome with the gleam of battle in your eye." She put her palms against Talbott's cheeks, pulled his head forward, and stretched her neck to kiss him on the lips—a quick one. "There!"

"Vic is going now," I told her. "Come on, Talbott, I'll let you out."

Before he came he enfolded Dorothy in his arms. I glanced at Safford, expecting him to counter by enfolding Audrey, but he was standing by with his fists still doubled up. So I herded Talbott out of the room ahead of me. In the hall, while he was getting his hat and coat, I took a look through the one-way panel, saw that the stoop was clear, and opened the door. As he crossed the sill I told him, "You go for the head too much. You'll break a hand that way someday."

Back in the office someone had righted the overturned chair, and they were all seated again. Apparently, though her knight had been given the boot, Dorothy was going to stick. As I crossed to resume my place at my desk Wolfe was saying, "We got interrupted, Miss Rooney. As I said, you seem to be the most vulnerable, since you were on the scene. Will you please move a little closer—that chair there? Archie, your notebook."

VI

At 10:55 the next morning I was sitting in the office—not still, but again—waiting for Wolfe to come down from the plant rooms on the roof, where he keeps ten thousand orchids and an assortment of other specimens of vegetation. I was playing three-handed pinochle with Saul Panzer and Orrie Cather, who had been phoned to come in for a job. Saul always wore an old brown cap, was undersized and homely, with a big nose, and was the best field man in the world for everything that could be done without a dinner jacket. Orrie, who would be able to get along without a hairbrush in a few years, was by no means up to Saul but was a good all-round man.

At 10:55 I was three bucks down.

In a drawer of my desk were two notebookfuls. Wolfe hadn't kept the clients all night, but there hadn't been much left of it when he let them go, and we now knew a good deal more about all of them than any of the papers had printed. In some respects they were all alike, as they told it. For instance, none of them had killed Sigmund Keyes; none was heartbroken over his death, not even his daughter; none had ever owned a revolver or knew much about shooting one; none could produce any evidence that would help to convict Talbott or even get him arrested; none had an airtight alibi; and each had a motive of his own which might not have been the best in the world, like Talbott's, but was nothing to sneeze at.

So they said.

Ferdinand Pohl had been indignant. He couldn't see why time should be wasted on them and theirs, since the proper and sole objective was to bust Talbott's alibi and nab him. But he came through with his facts. Ten years previously he had furnished the hundred thousand dollars that had been needed to get Sigmund Keyes started with the style of setup suitable for a big-time industrial designer. In the past couple of years the Keyes profits had been up above the clouds, and Pohl had wanted an even split and hadn't got it. Keyes had ladled out a measly annual five per cent on Pohl's ante, five thousand a year, whereas half the profits would have been ten times that, and Pohl couldn't confront him with the classic alternative, buy my share or sell me yours, because Pohl had been making bad guesses on other matters and was deep in debt. The law wouldn't have helped, since the partnership agreement had guaranteed Pohl only the five per cent and Keyes had given the profits an alias by taking the gravy as salary, claiming it was his designing ability that made the money. It had been, Pohl said, a case of misjudging a man's character. Now that Keyes was dead it would be a different story, with the contracts on hand and royalties to come for periods up to twenty years. If Pohl and Dorothy, who inherited, couldn't come to an understanding, it would be up to a judge to make the divvy, and Pohl would get, he thought, at least two hundred thousand, and probably a lot more.

He denied that that was a good motive for murder —not for him, and anyway it was silly to discuss it, because that Tuesday morning at 7:28 he had taken a train to Larchmont to sail his boat. Had he boarded the train at Grand Central or One Hundred and Twenty-fifth Street? Grand Central, he said. Had he been alone? Yes. He had left his apartment on East Eighty-fourth Street at seven o'clock and taken the subway. Did he often ride the subway? Yes, fairly frequently, when it wasn't a rush hour. And so on, for fourteen pages of a notebook. I gave him a D minus, even grant-ing that he could cinch it that he reached Larchmont on that train, since it would have stopped at One Hun-dred and Twenty-fifth Street at 7:38, ten minutes after it left Grand Central.

With Dorothy Keyes the big question was how much of the Keyes profits had been coming her way. Part of the time she seemed to have the idea that her father had been fairly liberal with the dough, and then she would toss in a comment which indicated that he had been as tight-fisted as a baby hanging onto an-other baby's toy. It was confusing because she had no head for figures. The conclusion I reached was that her take had averaged somewhere between five hundred and twenty thousand a year, which was a wide gap. The point was, which way was she sitting prettier, with her father alive and making plenty of dough and shelling it out, or with him dead and everything hers after Pohl had been attended to? She saw the point all right, and I must say it didn't seem to shock her much, since she didn't even bother to lift her brows.

If it was an act it was good. Instead of standing on

the broad moral principle that daughters do not kill fathers, her fundamental position was that at the unspeakable hour in question, half-past seven in the morning, she couldn't even have been killing a fly, let alone her father. She was never out of bed before eleven, except in emergencies, as for instance the Tuesday morning under discussion, when word had come sometime between nine and ten that her father was dead. That had roused her. She had lived with her father in an apartment on Central Park South. Servants? Two maids. Wolfe put it to her: would it have been possible, before seven in the morning, for her to leave the apartment and the building, and later get back in again, without being seen? Not, she declared, unless someone had turned a hose on her to wake her up; that accomplished, possibly the rest could be managed, but she really couldn't say because he had never tried.

I gave her no mark at all because by that time I was prejudiced and couldn't trust my judgment.

Frank Broadyke was a wow. He had enthusiastically adopted Talbott's suggestion that if he, Broadyke, had undertaken to kill anyone it would have been Talbott and not Keyes, since it implied that Keyes' eminence in his profession had been on account of Talbott's salesmanship instead of Keyes' ability as a designer. Broadyke liked that very much and kept going back to it and plugging it. He admitted that the steady decrease in his own volume of business had been coincident with the rise of Keyes', and he further admitted, when the matter was mentioned by Dorothy, that only three days before the murder Keyes had started an action at law against him for damages to the tune of a hundred thousand dollars, complaining that Broadyke had stolen designs from Keyes' office which had got him contracts for a concrete mixer and an electric washing machine. But what the hell, he maintained, the man he would naturally have it in for was Vic Talbott, who had stampeded the market with his high-pressure sales methods—and his personality. Ask any reputable industrial designer; ask all of them. Keyes had been a mediocre gadget contriver, with no real understanding of the intricate and intimate relationship between function and design. I see from my notebook that he permitted himself to say that four times altogether.

He had been doing his best to recover lost ground. He partook, he said, of the nature of the lark; the sunrise stirred and inspired him; that was his time of day. All his brilliant early successes had been conceived before the dew was dry in shady places. In the afternoon and evening he was no better than a clod. But eventually he had got lazy and careless, stayed up late and got up late, and it was then his star had begun to dim. Recently, quite recently, he had determined to light the flame again, and only a month ago he had started getting to his office before seven o'clock, three hours before the staff was due to arrive. To his satisfaction and delight, it was beginning to work. The flashes of inspiration were coming back. That very Tuesday morning, the morning Keyes was killed, he had greeted his staff when they arrived by showing them a revolutionary and irresistible design for an electric egg beater.

Had anyone, Wolfe wanted to know, been with him in his office that morning during the parturition, say from half-past six to eight o'clock? No. No one.

For alibi, Broadyke, of those three, came closest to being naked.

Since I had cottoned to Audrey Rooney and would

have married her any second if it wasn't that I
wouldn't want my wife to be a public figure and there
was her picture on the calendar on the wall of Sam's
Diner, it was a setback to learn that her parents in
Vermont had actually named her Annie, and she had
changed it herself. Okay if she hadn't cared for Annie
with Rooney, but good God, why Audrey? Audrey. It
showed a lack in her.

It did not, of course, indict her for murder, but her
tale helped out on that. She had worked in the Keyes
office as Victor Talbott's secretary, and a month ago
Keyes had fired her because he suspected her of swip-
ing designs and selling them to Broadyke. When she
had demanded proof and Keyes hadn't been able to
produce it, she had proceeded to raise hell, which I
could well believe. She had forced her way into his
private room at the office so often that he had been
compelled to hire a husky to keep her out. She had
tried to get the rest of the staff, forty of them, to walk
out on him until justice had been done her, and had
darned near succeeded. She had tried to get at him at
his home but failed. Eight days before his death, on a
Monday morning, he had found her waiting for him
when he arrived at the Stillwell Riding Academy to
get his four legs. With the help of the stable hand, by
name Wayne Safford, he had managed to mount and
clatter off for the park.

But next morning Annie Audrey was there again,
and the next one too. What was biting her hardest, as
she explained to Wolfe at the outset, was that Keyes
had refused to listen to her, had never heard her side,
and was so mean and stubborn he didn't intend to. She
thought he should. She didn't say in so many words
that another reason she kept on showing up at the
academy was that the stable hand didn't seem to mind,

but that could be gathered. The fourth morning, Thursday, Vic Talbott had arrived too, to accompany Keyes on his ride. Keyes, pestered by Audrey, had poked her in the belly with his crop; Wayne Safford had pushed Keyes hard enough to make him stumble and fall; Talbott had intervened and taken a swing at Wayne; and Wayne had socked Talbott and knocked him into a stall that hadn't been cleaned.

Evidently, I thought, Wayne held back when he was boxing in a nicely furnished office on a Kerman rug; and I also thought that if I had been Keyes I would have tried designing an electric horse for my personal use. But the next day he was back for more, and did get more comments from Audrey, but that was as far as it went; and three days later, Monday, it was the same. Talbott wasn't there either of those two days.

Tuesday morning Audrey got there at a quarter to six, the advantage of the early arrival being that she could make the coffee while Wayne curried horses. They ate cinnamon rolls with the coffee. Wolfe frowned at that because he hates cinnamon rolls. A little after six a phone call came from the Hotel Churchill not to saddle Talbott's horse and to tell Keyes he wouldn't be there. At six-thirty Keyes arrived, on the dot as usual, responded only with grimly tightened lips to Audrey's needling, and rode off. Audrey stayed on at the academy, was there continuously for another hour, and was still there at twenty-five minutes to eight, when Keyes' horse came wandering in under an empty saddle.

Was Wayne Safford also there continuously? Yes, they were together all the time.

So Audrey and Wayne were fixed up swell. When it came Wayne's turn he didn't contradict her on a single point, which I thought was very civilized behavior for a stable hand. He too made the mistake of mentioning cinnamon rolls, but otherwise turned in a perfect score.

When they had gone, more than two hours after midnight, I stood, stretched and yawned good, and told Wolfe, "Five mighty fine clients. Huh?"

He grunted in disgust and put his hands on the rim of his desk to push his chair back.

"I could sleep on it more productively," I stated, "if you would point. Not at Talbott, I don't need that. I'm a better judge of love looks than you are, and I saw him looking at Dorothy, and he has it bad. But the clients? Pohl?"

"He needs money, perhaps desperately, and now he'll get it."

"Broadyke?"

"His vanity was mortally wounded, his business was going downhill, and he was being sued for a large sum."

"Dorothy?"

"A daughter. A woman. It could have gone back to her infancy, or it could have been a trinket denied her today."

"Safford?"

"A primitive romantic. Within three days after he met that girl the fool was eating cinnamon rolls with her at six o'clock in the morning. What about his love look?"

I nodded. "Giddy."

"And he saw Mr. Keyes strike the girl with his riding crop."

"Not strike her, poke her."

"Even worse, because more contemptuous. Also

the girl had persuaded him that Mr. Keyes was persisting in a serious injustice to her."

"Okay, that'll do. How about her?"

"A woman either being wronged or caught wronging another. In either case, unhinged."

"Also he poked her with his crop."

"No," Wolfe disagreed. "Except in immediate and urgent retaliation, no woman ever retorts to physical violence from a man in kind. It would not be womanly. She devises subtleties." He got to his feet. "I'm sleepy." He started for the door.

Following, I told his back, "I know one thing, I would collect from every damn one of them in advance. I can't imagine why Cramer wanted to see them again, even Talbott, after a whole week with them. Why don't he throw in and draw five new cards? He's sore as a pup. Shall we phone him?"

"No." We were in the hall. Wolfe, heading for the elevator to ascend to his room on the second floor, turned. "What did he want?"

"He didn't say, but I can guess. He's at a dead stop in pitch-dark in the middle of a six corners, and he came to see if you've got a road map."

I made for the stairs, since the elevator is only four by six, and with all of Wolfe inside, it would already be cramped.

VII

"Forty trump," Orrie Cather said at 10:55 Wednesday morning.

I had told them the Keyes case had knocked on our door and we had five suspects for clients, and that was all. Wolfe had not seen fit to tell me what their errands would be, so I was entertaining at cards instead of summarizing the notebooks for them. At eleven sharp we ended the game, and Orrie and I shelled out to Saul, as usual, and a few minutes later the door from the hall opened and Wolfe entered. He greeted the two hired hands, got himself installed behind his desk, rang for beer, and asked me, "You've explained things to Saul and Orrie, of course?"

"Certainly not. For all I knew it's classified."

He grunted and told me to get Inspector Cramer. I dialed the number and had more trouble getting through than usual, finally had Cramer and signaled to Wolfe, and, since I got no sign to keep off, I stayed on. It wasn't much of a conversation.

"Mr. Cramer? Nero Wolfe."

"Yeah. What do you want?"

"I'm sorry I was busy last evening. It's always a pleasure to see you. I've been engaged in the matter of Mr. Keyes' death, and it will be to our mutual interest for you to let me have a little routine information."

"Like what?"

"To begin with, the name and number of the mounted policeman who saw Mr. Keyes in the park at ten minutes past seven that morning. I want to send Archie—"

"Go to hell." The connection went.

Wolfe hung up, reached for the beer tray which Fritz had brought in, and told me, "Get Mr. Skinner of the District Attorney's office."

I did so, and Wolfe got on again. In the past Skinner had had his share of moments of irritation with Wolfe, but at least he hadn't had the door slammed in his face the preceding evening and therefore was not boorish. When he learned that Wolfe was on the Keyes case he wanted to know plenty, but Wolfe stiff-armed him without being too rude and soon had what he was after. Upon Wolfe's assurance that he would keep Skinner posted on developments at his end, which they both knew was a barefaced lie, the Assistant D.A. even offered to ask headquarters to arrange for me to see the cop. And did so. In less than ten minutes after Wolfe and he were finished, a call came from Centre Street to tell me that Officer Hefferan would meet me at 11:45 at the corner of Sixty-sixth Street and Central Park West.

During the less than ten minutes, Wolfe had drunk beer, asked Saul about his family, and told me what I was expected to find out from the cop. That made me sore, but even more it made me curious. When we're on a case it sometimes happens that Wolfe gets the notion that I have got involved on some angle or with some member of the cast, and that therefore it is necessary to switch me temporarily onto a siding. I had about given up wasting nervous energy resenting it. But what was it this time? I had bought nobody's version and was absolutely fancy free, so why should he send me out to chew the rag with a cop and keep Saul and Orrie for more important errands? It was beyond me, and I was glaring at him and about to open up, when the phone rang again.

It was Ferdinand Pohl, asking for Wolfe. I was going to keep out of it, since the main attack was to be entrusted to others, but Wolfe motioned me to stay on.

"I'm at the Keyes office," Pohl said, "Forty-seventh and Madison. Can you come up here right away?"

"Certainly not," Wolfe said in a grieved tone. It always riled him that anybody in the world didn't know that he never left his house on business, and rarely for anything whatever. "I work only at home. What's the matter?"

"There's someone here I want you to talk to. Two members of the staff. With their testimony I can prove that Talbott took those designs and sold them to Broadyke. This clinches it that it was Talbott who killed Keyes. Of us five, the only ones that could possibly be suspected were Miss Rooney and that stable hand, with that mutual alibi they had, and this clears her—and him too, of course."

"Nonsense. It does nothing of the sort. It proves that she was unjustly accused of theft, and an unjust accusation rankles more than a just one. Now you can have Mr. Talbott charged with larceny, at least. I'm extremely busy. Thank you very much for calling. I shall need the cooperation of all of you."

Pohl wanted to prolong it, but Wolfe got rid of him, drank more beer, and turned to me. "You're expected there in twenty minutes, Archie, and considering your tendency to get arrested for speeding—"

I had had one ticket for speeding in eight years. I walked to the door but turned to remark bitterly, "If you think you're just sending me out to play, try again. Who was the last to see Keyes alive? The cop. He did it. And who will I deliver him to—you? No. Inspector Cramer!"

VIII

It was sunny and warm for October, and the drive uptown would have been pleasant if I hadn't been prejudiced by my feeling that I was being imposed on. Parking on Sixty-fifth Street, I walked around the corner and up a block, and crossed Central Park West to where a man in uniform was monkeying with his horse's bridle. I have met a pack of guardians of the peace on my rounds, but this rugged manly face with a pushed-in nose and bright big eyes was new to me. I introduced myself and showed credentials and said it was nice of him, busy as he was, to give me his time. Of course that was a blunder, but I've admitted I was prejudiced.

"Oh," he said, "one of our prominent kidders, huh?"

I made for cover. "About as prominent," I declared, "as a fish egg in a bowl of caviar."

"Oh, you eat caviar."

"Goddam it," I muttered, "let's start over again." I walked four paces to a lamp post, wheeled, returned to him, and announced, "My name's Goodwin and I work for Nero Wolfe. Headquarters said I could ask you a couple of questions and I'd appreciate it."

"Uh-huh. A friend of mine in the Fifteenth Squad has told me about you. You damn near got him sent to the marshes."

"Then you were already prejudiced. So was I, but not against you. Not even against your horse. Speaking of horses, that morning you saw Keyes on his horse, not long before he was killed, what time was it?"

"Ten minutes past seven."

"Within a minute or two?"

"Not within anything. Ten minutes past seven. I was on the early shift then, due to check out at eight. As you say, I'm so busy that I have no time, so I was hanging around expecting to see Keyes go by as per schedule. I liked to see his horse—a light chestnut with a fine spring to him."

"How did the horse look that morning—same as usual? Happy and healthy?" Seeing the look on his face, I added hastily, "I've sworn off kidding until to-morrow. I actually want to know, was it his horse?"

"Certainly it was! Maybe you don't know horses. I do."

"Okay. I used to too, when I was a boy on a farm in Ohio, but we haven't corresponded lately. What about Keyes that morning, did he look sick or well or mad or glad or what?"

"He looked as usual, nothing special."

"Did you speak to each other?"

"No."

"Had he shaved that morning?"

"Sure he had." Officer Hefferan was controlling himself. "He had used two razors, one on the right side and another one on the left, and he wanted to know which one did the best job, so he asked me to rub his cheeks and tell him what I thought."

"You said you didn't speak."

"Nuts."

"I agree. Let's keep this frankly hostile. I shouldn't have asked about shaving, I should have come right out and asked what I want to know, how close were you to him?"

"Two hundred and seventy feet."

"Oh, you've measured it?"

"I've paced it. The question came up."

"Would you mind showing me the spot? Where he was and where you were?"

"Yes, I'd mind, but I've got orders."

The courteous thing would have been for him to lead his horse and walk with me, so he didn't do that. He mounted his big bay and rode into the park, with me tagging along behind; and not only that, he must have given it a private signal that they mustn't be late. I never saw a horse walk so fast. He would have loved to lose me and blame it on me, or at least make me break into a trot, but I gave my legs the best stretch

they had had in years, bending my elbows and pump-
ing my lungs, and I wasn't more than thirty paces in
the rear when he finally came to a stop at the crest of a
little knoll. There were a lot of trees, big and little, off
to the right down the slope, and clumps of bushes were
on the left, but in between there was a good view of a
long stretch of the bridle path. It was almost at a right
angle to our line of vision, and at its nearest looked
about a hundred yards away.

He did not dismount. There is no easier way in the
world to feel superior to a man than to talk to him from
on top of a horse.

Speaking, I handled things so as not to seem out of
breath. "You were here?"

"Right here."

"And he was going north."

"Yep." He gestured. "That direction."

"You saw him. Did he see you?"

"Yes. He lifted his crop to me and I waved back. We
often did that."

"But he didn't stop or gaze straight at you."

"He didn't gaze straight or crooked. He was out for
a ride. Listen, brother." The mounted man's tone indicated that he had decided to humor me and get it over.
"I've been through all this with the Homicide boys. If
you're asking was it Keyes, it was. It was his horse. It
was his bright yellow breeches, the only ones that
color around, and his blue jacket and his black derby.
It was the way he sat, with his shoulders hunched and
his stirrups too long. It was Keyes."

"Good. May I pat your horse?"

"No."

"Then I won't. It would suit me fine if the occasion
arose someday for me to pat you. When I'm dining

with the inspector this evening I'll put in a word for you, not saying what kind."

I hoofed it out of the park and along Sixty-sixth Street to Broadway, found a drugstore and a phone booth, wriggled onto the stool, and dialed my favorite number. It was Orrie Cather's voice that answered. So, I remarked to myself, he's still there, probably sitting at my desk; Wolfe's instructions for him must be awful complicated. I asked for Wolfe and got him.

"Yes, Archie?"

"I am phoning as instructed. Officer Hefferan is a Goodwin-hater, but I swallowed my pride. On the stand he would swear up and down that he saw Keyes at the place and time as given, and I guess he did, but a good lawyer could shoot it full of ifs and buts."

"Why? Is Mr. Hefferan a shuttlecock?"

"By no means. He knows it all. But it wasn't a closeup."

"You'd better let me have it verbatim."

I did so. By years of practice I had reached the point where I could relay a two-hour conversation, without any notes but practically word for word, and the brief session I had just come from gave me no trouble at all. When I had finished Wolfe said, "Indeed."

Silence.

I waited a full two minutes and then said politely, "Please tell Orrie not to put his feet on my desk."

In another minute Wolfe's voice came. "Mr. Pohl has telephoned again, twice, from the Keyes office. He's a jackass. Go there and see him. The address—"

"I know the address. What part of him do I look at?"

"Tell him to stop telephoning me. I want it stopped."

"Right. I'll cut the wires. Then what do I do?"

"Phone in again and we'll see."

It clicked off. I wriggled off the stool and out of the booth and stood muttering to myself until I noticed that the line of girls on stools at the soda fountain, especially one of them with blue eyes and dimples, was rudely staring at me. I told her distinctly, "Meet me at Tiffany's ring counter at two o'clock," and strode out. Since I wouldn't be able to park within a mile of Forty-seventh and Madison, I decided to leave my car where it was and snare a taxi.

IX

One quick look around the Keyes establishment on the twelfth floor was enough to show where a good slice of the profits had gone, unless that was what Pohl's hundred grand had been used for. Panels of four kinds of blond wood made up both the walls and ceiling, and the furniture matched. The seats of the chairs for waiting callers were upholstered in blue and black super-burlap, and you had to watch yourself on the rugs not to twist an ankle. Everywhere, in glass cases against the walls, on pedestals scattered around, and on platforms and tables, were models of almost anything you could think of, from fountain pens to airplanes.

When a woman with pink earrings learned that I sought Mr. Pohl she gave me a wary and reproachful look, but she functioned. After a little delay I was waved through a door and found myself at the end of a long wide corridor. There was no one in sight and I had been given no directions, so it was a case of hide and seek. The best opening move seemed to be to walk down the corridor, so I started, glancing into open doors on either side as I passed. The same scale of interior architecture seemed to prevail throughout, with wide variations in style and color. At the fourth door on the right I saw him, and he called to me, simultaneously.

"Come in, Goodwin!"

I entered. It was a big room with three wide windows, and at a quick glance appeared to be the spot where they had really decided to spread themselves. The rugs were white and the walls were black, and the enormous desk that took all of one end was either ebony or call in an expert. The chair behind the desk, in which Pohl was seated, was likewise.

"Where's Wolfe?" Pohl demanded.

"Where he always is," I replied, negotiating rugs. "At home, sitting down."

He was scowling at me. "I thought he was with you. When I phoned him a few minutes ago he intimated that he might be. He's not coming?"

"No. Never. I'm glad you phoned him again because, as he told you this morning in my hearing, he'll need the cooperation of all of you."

"He'll get mine," Pohl stated grimly. "Since he's not coming for it himself, I suppose I ought to give this to you." He took papers from his breast pocket, looked through them, selected one and held it out. I stepped to the desk to take it.

It was a single sheet, with "Memo from Sigmund Keyes" on it, printed fancy, and scrawled in ink was a list of towns:

> Dayton, Ohio Aug. 11 & 12
> Boston Aug. 21
> Los Angeles Aug. 27 to Sept. 5
> Meadville, Pa. Sept. 15

Pittsburgh Sept. 16 & 17
Chicago Sept. 24–26
Philadelphia Oct. 1

"Much obliged," I thanked him, and stuck it in my pocket. "Covers a lot of country."

Pohl nodded. "Talbott gets around, and he's a good salesman, I admit that. Tell Wolfe I did just as he said, and I got it out of a record right here in Keyes' desk, so no one knows anything about it. Those are all the out-of-town trips Talbott has made since August first. I have no idea what Wolfe wants it for, but by God it shows he's on the job, and whoever does know what a detective is after? I don't give a damn how mysterious it is as long as I can help him get Talbott."

I had an eye cocked at him, trying to decide whether he was really as naïve as he sounded. It gave me one on Wolfe, knowing that he had tried to keep Pohl away from a phone by giving him work to do, and here Pohl had cleaned it up in no time at all and was ready to ask for more. But instead of asking Wolfe for more, he asked me. He shot it at me.

"Go out and get me some sandwiches and coffee. There's a place on Forty-sixth Street, Perrine's."

I sat down. "That's funny, I was about to ask you to get me some. I'm tired and hungry. Let's go together."

"How the hell can I?" he demanded.

"Why not?"

"Because I might not be able to get in again. This is Keyes' room, but Keyes is dead, and I own part of this business and I've got a right here! Dorothy has tried to chase me out—damn her, she used to sit on my lap! I want certain information, and she has ordered the staff not to give me any. She threatened to get the police to put me out, but she won't do that. She's had enough of the police this last week." Pohl was scowling at me. "I prefer corned beef, and the coffee black, no sugar."

I grinned at his scowl. "So you're squatting. Where's Dorothy?"

"Down the hall, in Talbott's room."

"Is Talbott there?"

"No, he hasn't been in today."

I glanced at my wrist and saw twenty minutes past one. I stood up. "Rye with mustard?"

"No. White bread and nothing on it—no butter."

"Okay. On one condition, that you promise not to phone Mr. Wolfe. If you did you'd be sure to tell him that you got what he's after, and I want to surprise him with it."

He said he wouldn't, and that he wanted two sandwiches and plenty of coffee, and I departed. Two men and a woman who were standing in the corridor, talking, inspected me head to foot as I passed but didn't try to trip me, and I went on out to the elevators, descended, and got directed to a phone booth in the lobby.

Orrie Cather answered again, and I began to suspect that he and Saul were continuing the pinochle game with Wolfe.

"I'm on my way," I told Wolfe when he was on, "to get corned-beef sandwiches for Pohl and me but I've got a plan. He promised not to phone you while I'm gone, and if I don't go back he's stuck. He has installed himself in Keyes' room, which you ought to see, against Dorothy's protests, and intends to stay. Been there all day. What shall I do, come home or go to a movie?"

"Has Mr. Pohl had lunch?"

"Certainly not. That's what the sandwiches are for."

"Then you'll have to take them to him."

I remained calm because I knew he meant it from his heart, or at least his stomach. He couldn't bear the idea of even his bitterest enemy missing a meal.

"All right," I conceded, "and I may get a tip. By the way, that trick you tried didn't work. Right away he found a record of Talbott's travels in Keyes' desk and copied it off on a sheet from Keyes' memo pad. I've got it in my pocket."

"Read it to me."

"Oh, you can't wait." I got the paper out and read the list of towns and dates to him. Twice he said I was going too fast, so apparently he was taking it down. When that farce was over I asked, "After I feed him, then what?"

"Call in again when you've had your lunch."

I banged the thing on the hook.

X

They were good sandwiches. The beef was tender and full of hot salty sap, with just the right amount of fat, and the bread had some character. I was a little short on milk, having got only a pint, but stretched it out. In between bites we discussed matters, and I made a mistake. I should of course have told Pohl nothing whatever, especially since the more I saw of him the less I liked him, but the sandwiches were so good that I got careless and let it out that as far as I knew no attack had been made on the phone girl and the waiter at the Hotel Churchill. Pohl was determined to phone Wolfe immediately to utter a howl, and in order to stop him I had to tell him that Wolfe had other men on the case and I didn't know who or what they were covering.

I was about to phone myself when the door opened and Dorothy Keyes and Victor Talbott walked in.

I stood up. Pohl didn't.

"Hello hello," I said cheerfully. "Nice place you have here."

Neither of them even nodded to me. Dorothy dropped into a chair against a wall, crossed her legs, and turned her gaze on Pohl with her chin in the air.

Talbott marched over to us at the ebony desk, stopped at my elbow, and told Pohl, "You know damn well you've got no right here, going through things and trying to order the staff around. You have no right here at all. I'll give you one minute to get out."

"*You'll* give me?" Pohl sounded nasty and looked nasty. "You're a paid employee, and you won't be that long, and I'm part owner, and you say *you'll* give me! Trying to order the staff around, am I? I'm giving the staff a chance to tell the truth, and they're doing it. Two of them have spent an hour in a lawyer's office, getting it on paper. A complaint has been sworn against Broadyke for receiving stolen goods, and he's been arrested by now."

Talbott said, "Get out," without raising his voice.

Pohl, not moving, said, "And I might also mention that a complaint has been sworn against you for stealing the goods. The designs you sold to Broadyke. Are you going to try to alibi that too?"

Talbott's jaw worked a couple of seconds before it let his lips open for speech. His teeth stayed together as he said, "You can leave now."

"Or I can stay. I'll stay." Pohl was sneering, and it made his network of face creases deeper. "You may have noticed I'm not alone."

I didn't care for that. "Just a minute," I put in. "I'll hold your coats, and that's all. Don't count on me, Mr.

Pohl. I'm strictly a spectator, except for one thing, you haven't paid me for your sandwiches and coffee. Ninety-five cents before you go, if you're going."

"I'm not going. It's different here from what it was in the park that morning, Vic. There's a witness."

Talbott took two quick steps, used a foot to shove the big ebony chair back free of the desk, made a grab in the neighborhood of Pohl's throat, got his necktie, and jerked him out of the chair. Pohl came forward and tried to come up at the same time, but Talbott, moving fast, kept going with him, dragging him around the corner of the desk.

I had got upright and backed off, not to be in the way.

Suddenly Talbott went down, flat on his back, an upflung hand gripping a piece of the necktie. Pohl was not very springy, even for his age, but he did his best. He scrambled to his feet, started yelling, "Help! Police! Help!" at the top of his voice, and seized the chair I had been sitting on and raised it high. His idea was to drop it on the prostrate enemy, and my leg muscles tightened for quick action, but Talbott leaped up and yanked the chair away from him. Pohl ran. He scooted around behind the desk, and Talbott went after him. Pohl, yelling for help again, slid around the other end, galloped across the room to a table which held a collection of various objects, picked up an electric iron, and threw it. Missing Talbott, who dodged, it crashed onto the ebony desk and knocked the telephone to the floor. Apparently having an iron thrown at him made Talbott mad, for when he reached Pohl, instead of trying to get a hold on something more substantial than a necktie, he hauled off and landed on his jaw, in spite of the warning I had given him the day before.

"Off of that, you!" a voice boomed.

Glancing to the right, I saw two things: first, that
Dorothy, still in her chair, hadn't even uncrossed her
legs, and second, that the law who had entered was not
a uniformed pavement man but a squad dick I knew by
sight. Evidently he had been somewhere around the
premises, but it was the first I had seen of him.

He crossed to the gladiators. "This is no way to
act," he declared.

Dorothy, moving swiftly, was beside him. "This
man," she said, indicating Pohl, "forced his way in here
and was told to leave but wouldn't. I am in charge of
this place and he has no right here. I want a charge
against him for trespassing or disturbing the peace or
whatever it is. He tried to kill Mr. Talbott with a chair
and then with that iron he threw at him."

I, having put the phone back on the desk, had wandered near, and the law gave me a look.

"What were you doing, Goodwin, trimming your
nails?"

"No, sir," I said respectfully, "it was just that I
didn't want to get stepped on."

Talbott and Pohl were both speaking at once.

"I know, I know," the dick said, harassed. "Ordinarily, with people like you, I would feel that the thing
to do was to sit down and discuss it, but with what
happened to Keyes things are different from ordinary." He appealed to Dorothy. "You say you're making a charge, Miss Keyes?"

"I certainly am."

"So am I," Talbott stated.

"Then that's that. Come along with me, Mr. Pohl."

"I'm staying here." Pohl was still panting. "I have a
right here and I'm staying here."

"No, you're not. You heard what the lady said."

"Yes, but you didn't hear what I said. I was assaulted. She makes a charge. So do I. I was sitting quietly in a chair, not moving, and Talbott tried to strangle me, and he struck me. Didn't you see him strike me?"

"It was in self-defense," Dorothy declared. "You threw an iron—"

"To save my life! He assaulted—"

"All I did—"

"Hold it," the law said curtly. "Under the circumstances you can't talk yourselves into anything with me. You men will come along with me, both of you. Where's your hats and coats?"

They went. First they used up more breath on words and gestures, but they went, Pohl in the lead, with only half a necktie, Talbott next, and the law in the rear.

Thinking I might as well tidy up a little, I went and righted the chair Pohl had tried to use, then retrieved the iron and put it back on the table, and then examined the beautiful surface of the desk to see how much damage had been done.

"I suppose you're a coward, aren't you?" Dorothy inquired.

She had sat down again, in the same chair, and crossed the same legs. They were all right; I had no kick coming there.

"It's controversial," I told her, "It was on the Town Meeting of the Air last week. With a midget, if he's unarmed, I'm as brave as a lion. Or with a woman. Try picking on me. But with—" A buzz sounded.

"The phone," Dorothy said.

I pulled it to me and got the receiver to my ear.

"Is Miss Keyes there?"

"Yes," I said, "she's busy sitting down. Any message?"

"Tell her Mr. Donaldson is here to see her."

I did so, and for the first time saw an expression that was unquestionably human on Dorothy's face. At sound of the name Donaldson all trace of the brow-lifter vanished. Muscles tightened all over and color went. She may or may not have been what she had just called me, I didn't know because I had never seen or heard of Donaldson, but she sure was scared stiff.

I got tired waiting and repeated it. "Mr. Donaldson is here to see you."

"I—" She wet her lips. In a moment she swallowed. In another moment she stood up, said in a voice not soft at all, "Tell her to send him to Mr. Talbott's room," and went.

I forwarded the command as instructed, asked for an outside line, and, when I heard the dial tone, fingered the number. My wrist watch said five past three, and it stopped my tongue for a second when once more I heard Orrie's voice.

"Archie," I said shortly. "Let me speak to Saul."

"Saul? He's not here. Been gone for hours."

"Oh, I thought it was a party. Then Wolfe."

Wolfe's voice came. "Yes, Archie?"

"I'm in Keyes' office, sitting at his desk. I'm alone. I brought Pohl his lunch, and he owes me ninety-five cents. It just occurred to me that I've seen you go to great lengths to keep your clients from being arrested. Remember the time you buried Clara Fox in a box of osmundine and turned the hose on her? Or the time—"

"What about it?"

"They're scooping up all the clients, that's all. Broadyke has been collared for receiving stolen goods —the designs he bought from Talbott. Pohl has been pulled in for disturbing the peace, and Talbott for assault and battery. Not to mention that Miss Keyes has just had the daylights scared out of her."

"What are you talking about? What happened?"

I told him and, since he had nothing to do but sit and let Orrie answer the phone for him, I left nothing out. When I was through I offered the suggestion that it might be a good plan for me to stick around and find out what it was about Mr. Donaldson that made young women tremble and turn pale at sound of his name.

"No, I think not," Wolfe said, "unless he's a tailor. Just find out if he's a tailor, but discreetly. No disclosure. If so, get his address. Then find Miss Rooney— wait, I'll give you her address—"

"I know her address."

"Find her. Get her confidence. Get alone with her. Loosen up her tongue."

"What am I after—no, I know what I'm after. What are you after?"

"I don't know. Anything you can get. Confound it, you know what a case like this amounts to, there's nothing for it but trial and error—"

Movement over by the door had caught my eye, and I focused on it. Someone had entered and was approaching me.

"Okay," I told Wolfe. "There's no telling where she is, but I'll find her if it takes all day and all night." I hung up and grinned at the newcomer and greeted her.

"Hello, Miss Rooney. Looking for me?"

XI

Annie Audrey was all dressed up in a neat brown wool dress with red threads showing on it in little knots, but she didn't look pleased with herself or with anyone

else. You wouldn't think a face with all that pink skin
could look so sour. With no greeting, not even a nod,
she demanded as she approached, "How do you get to
see a man that's been arrested?"

"That depends," I told her. "Don't snap at me like
that. I didn't arrest him. Who do you want to see,
Broadyke?"

"No." She dropped onto a chair as if she needed
support quick. "Wayne Safford."

"Arrested what for?"

"I don't know. I saw him at the stable this morning
and then I went downtown to see about a job. A while
ago I phoned Lucy, my best friend here, and she told
me there was talk about Vic Talbott selling those designs to Broadyke, so I came to find out what was
happening and when I learned that Talbott and Pohl
had both been arrested I phoned Wayne to tell him
about it, and the man there answered and said a policeman had come and taken Wayne with him."

"For why?"

"The man didn't know. How do I get to see him?"

"You probably don't."

"But I have to!"

I shook my head. "You believe you have to, and I
believe you have to, but the cops won't. It depends on
what his invitation said. If they just want to consult
him about sweating horses he may be home in an hour.
If they've got a hook in him, or think they have, God
knows. You're not a lawyer or a relative."

She sat and looked at me, sourer than ever. In a
minute she spoke, bitterly. "You said yesterday I may
be nice."

"Meaning I should mount my bulldozer and move
heaven and earth?" I shook my head again. "Even if
you were so nice it made my head swim, the best I

could do for you this second would be to hold your hand, and judging from your expression that's not what you have in mind. Would you mind telling me what you have got in your mind besides curiosity?"

She got up, circled two corners of the desk to reach the phone, put it to her ear, and in a moment told the transmitter, "This is Audrey, Helen. Would you get me —No. Forget it."

She hung up, perched on a corner of the desk, and started giving me the chilly eye again, this time slanting down instead of up.

"It's me," she declared.

"What is?"

"This trouble. Wherever I am there's trouble."

"Yeah, the world's full of it. Wherever anybody is there's trouble. You get shaky ideas. Yesterday you were scared because you thought they were getting set to hang a murder on you, and not one of them has even hinted at it. Maybe you're wrong again."

"No, I'm not." She sounded grim. "There was that business of accusing me of stealing those designs. They didn't have to pick me for that, but you notice they did. Now all of a sudden that's cleared up, I'm out of that, and what happens? Wayne gets arrested for murder. Next thing—"

"I thought you didn't know what they took him for."

"I don't. But you'll see. He was with me, wasn't he?" She slid off the desk and was erect. "I think—I'm pretty sure—I'm going to see Dorothy Keyes."

"She's busy with a caller."

"I know it, but he may be gone."

"A man named Donaldson, and I'm wondering about him. I have a hunch Miss Keyes is starting a little investigation on her own. Do you happen to know if this Donaldson is a detective?"

"I know he isn't. He's a lawyer and a friend of Mr. Keyes. I've seen him here several times. Do you—"

What interrupted her was a man coming in the door and heading for us.

It was a man I had known for years. "We're busy," I told him brusquely. "Come back tomorrow."

I should have had sense enough to give up kidding Sergeant Purley Stebbins of the Homicide Squad long ago, since it always glanced off and rolled away. When he got sore, as he often did, it wasn't at the kidding but at what he considered my interference with the performance of his duty.

"So you're here," he stated.

"Yep. Miss Rooney, this is Sergeant—"

"Oh, I've met him before." Her face was just as sour at him as it had been at me.

"Yeah, we've met," Purley acquiesced. His honest brown eyes were at her. "I've been looking for you, Miss Rooney."

"Oh, my Lord, more questions?"

"The same ones. Just checking up. You remember that statement you signed, where you said that Tuesday morning you were at the riding academy with Safford from a quarter to six until after half-past seven, and both of you were there all the time? You remember that?"

"Certainly I do."

"Do you want to change it now?"

Audrey frowned. "Change what?"

"Your statement."

"Of course not. Why should I?"

"Then how do you account for the fact that you were seen riding a horse into the park during that period, and Safford, on another horse, was with you, and Safford has admitted it?"

"Count ten," I snapped at her, "before you answer. Or even a hun—"

"Shut up," Purley snarled. "How do you account for it, Miss Rooney? You must have figured this might come and got something ready for it. What's the answer?"

Audrey had left her perch on the desk to get on her feet and face the pursuer. "Maybe," she suggested, "someone couldn't see straight. Who says he saw us?"

"Okay." Purley hauled a paper from his pocket and unfolded it. He looked at me. "We're careful about these little details when that fat boss of yours has got his nose in." He held the paper so Audrey could see it. "This is a warrant for your arrest as a material witness. Your friend Safford wanted to read his clear through. Do you?"

She ignored his generous offer. "What does it mean?" she demanded.

"It means you're going to ride downtown with me."

"It also means—" I began.

"Shut up." Purley moved a step. His hand started for her elbow, but didn't reach it, for she drew back and then turned and was on her way. He followed and was at her heels as she went out the door. Apparently she thought she had found a way to get to see her Wayne.

I sat a little while with my lips screwed up, gazing at the ashtray on the desk. I shook my head at nothing in particular, just the state of things, reached for the phone, got an outside line, and dialed again.

Wolfe's voice answered.

"Where's Orrie?" I demanded. "Taking a nap on my bed?"

"Where are you?" Wolfe inquired placidly.

"Still in Keyes' office. More of the same. Two more gone."

"Two more what? Where?"

"Clients. In the hoosegow. We're getting awful low—"

"Who and why?"

"Wayne Safford and Audrey Rooney." I told him what had happened, without bothering to explain that Audrey had walked in before our previous conversation had ended. At the end I added, "So four out of five have been snaffled, and Talbott too. We're in a fine fix. That leaves us with just one, Dorothy Keyes, and it wouldn't surprise me if she was also on her way, judging from the look on her face when she heard who was— Hold it a minute."

What stopped me was the sight of another visitor entering the room. It was Dorothy Keyes. I told the phone, "I'll call back," hung up, and left my chair.

Dorothy came to me. She was still human, more so if anything. The perky lift of her was completely gone, the color scheme of her visible skin was washed-out gray, and her eyes were pinched with trouble.

"Mr. Donaldson gone?" I asked her.

"Yes."

"It's a bad day all around. Now Miss Rooney and Wayne Safford have been pinched. The police seem to think they left out something about that Tuesday morning. I was just telling Mr. Wolfe when you came—"

"I want to see him," she said.

"Who? Mr. Wolfe?"

"Yes. Immediately."

"What about?"

I'll be damned if her brows didn't go up. The humanity I thought I had seen was only on the surface.

"I'll tell him that," she stated, me being mud. "I must see him at once."

"You can't, not at once," I told her. "You could rush there in a taxi, but you might as well wait till I go to Sixty-fifth Street and get my car, because it's after four o'clock and he's up with the orchids, and he wouldn't see you until six even though you are the only client he's got still out of jail."

"But this is urgent!"

"Not for him it isn't, not until six o'clock. Unless you want to tell me about it. I'm permitted upstairs. Do you?"

"No."

"Then shall I go get my car?"

"Yes."

I went.

XII

At three minutes past six Wolfe, down from the plant rooms, joined us in the office. By the time Dorothy and I had got there she had made it perfectly plain that as far as I was concerned she was all talked out, our conversation during the ride downtown having consisted of her saying at one point, "Look out for that truck," and me replying, "I'm driving," so during the hour's wait I hadn't even asked her if she wanted a drink. And when Wolfe had entered and greeted her, and got his bulk adjusted in his chair behind his desk, the first thing she said was, "I want to speak to you privately."

Wolfe shook his head. "Mr. Goodwin is my confidential assistant, and if he didn't hear it from you he soon would from me. What is it?"

"But this is very—personal."

"Most things said in this room by visitors are. What is it?"

"There is no one I can go to but you." Dorothy was in one of the yellow chairs, facing him, leaning forward to him. "I don't know where I stand, and I've got to find out. A man is going to tell the police that I forged my father's name to a check. Tomorrow morning."

Her face was human again, with her eyes pinched.

"Did you?" Wolfe asked.

"Forge the check? Yes."

I lifted my brows.

"Tell me about it," Wolfe said.

It came out, and was really quite simple. Her father hadn't given her enough money for the style to which she wanted to accustom herself. A year ago she had forged a check for three thousand dollars, and he had of course discovered it and had received her promise that she would never repeat. Recently she had forged another one, this time for five thousand dollars, and her father had been very difficult about it, but there had been no thought in his head of anything so drastic as having his daughter arrested.

Two days after his discovery of this second offense he had been killed. He had left everything to his daughter, but had made a lawyer named Donaldson executor of the estate, not knowing, according to Dorothy, that Donaldson hated her. And now Donaldson had found the forged check among Keyes' papers, with a memorandum attached to it in Keyes' handwriting, and had called on Dorothy that afternoon to tell her that it was his duty, both as a citizen and as a lawyer, considering the manner of Keyes' death, to give the facts to the police. It was an extremely painful duty, he had asserted, but he would just have to grin and bear it.

I will not say that I smirked as I got these sordid facts scratched into my notebook, but I admit that I had no difficulty in keeping back the tears.

Wolfe, having got answers to all the questions that had occurred to him, leaned back and heaved a sigh. "I can understand," he murmured, "that you felt impelled to get rid of this nettle by passing it on to someone. But even if I grasped it for you, what then? What do I do with it?"

"I don't know." It is supposed to make people feel better to tell their troubles, but apparently it made Dorothy feel worse. She sounded as forlorn as she looked.

"Moreover," Wolfe went on, "what are you afraid of? The property, including the bank balance, now belongs to you. It would be a waste of time and money for the District Attorney's office to try to get you indicted and brought to trial, and it wouldn't even be considered. Unless Mr. Donaldson is an idiot he knows that. Tell him so. Tell him I say he's a nincompoop." Wolfe wiggled a finger at her. "Unless he thinks you killed your father and wants to help get you electrocuted. Does he hate you that much?"

"He hates me," Dorothy said harshly, "all he can."

"Why?"

"Because once I let him think I might marry him, and he announced it, and then I changed my mind. He has strong feelings. It was strong when he loved me, and it is just as strong now when he hates me. Any way he can use that check to hurt me, he'll do it."

"Then you can't stop him, and neither can I. The forged check and your father's memorandum are le-

gally in his possession, and nothing can keep him from
showing them to the police. Does he ride horseback?"

"Oh, my God," Dorothy said hopelessly. She stood
up. "I thought you were clever! I thought you would
know what to do!" She made for the door, but at the
sill she turned. "You're just a cheap shyster too! I'll
handle the dirty little rat myself!"

I got up and went to the hall to let her out, to make
sure that the door was properly closed behind her.
When I was back in the office I sat down and tossed
the notebook into a drawer and remarked, "Now she's
got us all tagged. I'm a coward, you're a shyster, and
the executor of her father's estate is a rat. That poor
kid needs some fresh contacts."

Wolfe merely grunted, but it was a good-humored
grunt, for the dinner hour was near, and he never per-
mits himself to get irritated just before a meal.

"So," I said, "unless she does some fancy handling
in a hurry she will be gathered in before noon tomorrow, and she was the last we had. All five of them, and
also the suspect we were supposed to pin it on. I hope
Saul and Orrie are doing better than we are. I have a
date for dinner and a show with a friend, but I can
break it if there's anything I can be doing—"

"Nothing, thank you."

I glared at him. "Oh, Saul and Orrie are doing it?"

"There's nothing for this evening, for you. I'll be
here, attending to matters."

Yes, he would. He would be here, reading books,
drinking beer, and having Fritz tell anyone who called
that he was engaged. It wasn't the first time he had
decided that a case wasn't worth the effort and to hell
with it. On such occasions my mission was to keep after him until I had him jarred loose, but this time my
position was that if Orrie Cather could spend the after-

noon in my chair he could damn well do my work. So I let it lay and went up to my room to redecorate for the evening out.

It was a very nice evening on all counts. Dinner at Lily Rowan's, while not up to the standard Fritz had got my palate trained to, was always good. So was the show, and so was the dance band at the Flamingo Club, where we went afterward to get better acquainted, since I had only known her seven years. What with this and that I didn't get home until after three o'clock, and, following routine, looked in at the office to jiggle the handle of the safe and glance around. If there was a message for me Wolfe always left it on my desk under a paperweight, and there one was, on a sheet from his pad, in his small thin handwriting that was as easy to read as type.

I ran through it.

AG: Your work on the Keyes case has been quite satisfactory. Now that it is solved, you may proceed as arranged and go to Mr. Hewitt's place on Long Island in the morning to get those plants. Theodore will have the cartons ready for you. Don't forget to watch the ventilation.

NW

I read it through again and turned it over to look at the back, to see if there was another installment, but it was blank.

I sat at my desk and dialed a number. None of my closest friends or enemies was there, but I got a sergeant I knew named Rowley, and asked him, "On the Keyes case, do you need anything you haven't got?"

"Huh?" He always sounded hoarse. "We need everything. Send it C.O.D."

"A guy told me you had it on ice."

"Aw, go to bed."

He was gone. I sat a moment and then dialed again, the number of the *Gazette* office. Lon Cohen had gone home, but one of the journalists told me that as far as they knew the Keyes case was still back on a shelf, collecting dust.

I crumpled Wolfe's message and tossed it in the wastebasket, muttered, "The damn fat faker," and went up to bed.

XIII

In the Thursday morning papers there wasn't a single word in the coverage of the Keyes case to indicate that anyone had advanced even an inch in the hot pursuit of the murderer.

And I spent the whole day, from ten to six, driving to Lewis Hewitt's place on Long Island, helping to select and clean and pack ten dozen yearling plants, and driving back again. I did no visible fuming, but you can imagine my state of mind, and on my way home, when a cop stopped me as I was approaching Queensboro Bridge, and actually went so low as to ask me where the fire was, I had to get my tongue between my teeth to keep myself from going witty on him.

While I was lugging the last carton of plants up the stoop I had a surprise. A car I had often seen before, with PD on it, rolled up to the curb and stopped behind the sedan, and Inspector Cramer emerged from it.

"What has Wolfe got now?" he demanded, coming up the steps to me.

"A dozen zygopetalum," I told him coldly, "a dozen renanthera, a dozen odontoglossum—"

"Let me by," he said rudely.

I did so.

What I should have done, to drive it in that I was now a delivery boy and not a detective, was to go on helping Theodore get the orchids upstairs, and I set my teeth and started to do that, but it wasn't long before Wolfe's bellow came from the office. "Archie!"

I went on in. Cramer was in the red leather chair with an unlighted cigar tilted toward the ceiling by the grip of his teeth. Wolfe, his tightened lips showing that he was enjoying a quiet subdued rage, was frowning at him.

"I'm doing important work," I said curtly.

"It can wait. Get Mr. Skinner on the phone. If he has left his office, get him at home."

I would have gone to much greater lengths if Cramer hadn't been there. As it was, all I did was snort as I crossed to my desk and sat down and started to dial.

"Cut it!" Cramer barked savagely.

I went on dialing.

"I said stop it!"

"That will do, Archie," Wolfe told me. I turned from the phone and saw he was still frowning at the inspector but his lips had relaxed. He used them for speech. "I don't see, Mr. Cramer, what better you can ask than the choice I offer. As I told you on the phone, give me your word that you'll cooperate with me on my terms, and I shall at once tell you about it in full detail, including of course the justification for it. Or refuse to give me your word, that's the alternative, and I shall ask Mr. Skinner if the District Attorney's office would like to cooperate with me. I guarantee only that no harm will be done, but my expectation is that the case will be closed. Isn't that fair enough?"

Cramer growled like a tiger in a cage having a chair poked at him.

"I don't understand," Wolfe declared, "why the devil I bother with you. Mr. Skinner would jump at it."

Cramer's growl became words. "When would it be —tonight?"

"I said you'd get details after I get your promise, but you may have that much. It would be early tomorrow morning, contingent upon delivery of a package I'm expecting—by the way, Archie, you didn't put the car in the garage?"

"No, sir."

"Good. You'll have to go later, probably around midnight, to meet an airplane. It depends on the airplane, Mr. Cramer. If it arrives tomorrow instead of tonight, we'd have to postpone it until Saturday morning."

"Where? Here in your office?"

Wolfe shook his head. "That's one of the details you'll get. Confound it, do I mean what I say?"

"Search me. I never know. You say you'll take my word. Why not take my word that I'll either do it or forget I ever heard it?"

"No. Archie, get Mr. Skinner."

Cramer uttered a word that was for men only. "You and your goddam charades," he said bitterly. "Why do you bother with me? You know damn well I'm not going to let you slip it to the D.A.'s office, because you may really have it. You have before. Okay. On your terms."

Wolfe nodded. The gleam in his eye came and went so fast that it nearly escaped even me.

"Your notebook, Archie. This is rather elaborate, and I doubt if we can finish before dinner."

XIV

"I'll explain gladly," I told Officer Hefferan, "if you'll descend from that horse and get level with me. That's the democratic way to do it. Do you want me to get a stiff neck, slanting up at you?"

I yawned wide without covering it, since there was nothing there but nature and a mounted cop. Being up and dressed and breakfasted and outdoors working at seven in the morning was not an all-time record for me, but it was unusual, and I had been up late three nights in a row: Tuesday the congregation of clients, Wednesday the festivities with Lily Rowan, and Thursday the drive to La Guardia to meet the airplane, which had been on schedule.

Hefferan came off his high horse and was even with me. We were posted on top of the little knoll in Central Park to which he had led me the day I had made his acquaintance. It promised to be another warm October day. A little breeze was having fun with the leaves on the trees and bushes, and birds were darting and hopping around, discussing their plans for the morning.

"All I'm doing," Hefferan said to make it plain, "is obeying orders. I was told to meet you here and listen to you."

I nodded. "And you don't care for it. Neither do I, you stiff-backed Cossack, but I've got orders too. The setup is like this. As you know, down there behind that forest"—I pointed—"is a tool shed. Outside the shed Keyes' chestnut horse, saddled and bridled, is being held by one of your colleagues. Inside the shed there are two women named Keyes and Rooney, and four men named Pohl, Talbott, Safford, and Broadyke. Also Inspector Cramer is there with a detachment from his squad. One of the six civilians, chosen by secret ballot, is at this moment changing his or her clothes, putting on bright yellow breeches and a blue jacket, just like the outfit Keyes wore. Between you and me and your horse, the choosing was a put-up job, handled by Inspector Cramer. Dressed like Keyes, the chosen one is going to mount Keyes' horse and ride along that stretch of the bridle path, with shoulders hunched and stirrups too long, catch sight of you, and lift his or her crop to you in greeting. Your part is to be an honest man. Pretend it's not me telling you this, but someone you dearly love like the Police Commissioner. You are asked to remember that what you were interested in seeing was the horse, not the rider, and to put the question to yourself, did you actually recognize Keyes that morning, or just the horse and the getup?"

I appealed to him earnestly. "And for God's sake don't say a word to me. You wouldn't admit anything whatever to me, so keep your trap shut and save it for later, for your superiors. A lot depends on you, which may be regrettable, but it can't be helped now.

"If it won't offend you for me to explain the theory of it, it's this: The murderer, dressed like Keyes but covered with a topcoat, was waiting in the park uptown behind that thicket at half-past six, when Keyes first rode into the park and got onto the bridle path. If he had shot Keyes out of the saddle from a distance, even a short one, the horse would have bolted, so he stepped out and stopped Keyes, and got hold of the bridle before he pulled the trigger. One bullet for one. Then he dragged the body behind the thicket so it couldn't be seen from the bridle path, since another early-morning rider might come along, took off his topcoat—or maybe a thin raincoat—and stuffed it under his jacket, mounted the horse, and went for a ride through the park. He took his time so as to keep to Keyes' customary schedule. Thirty minutes later, approaching that spot"—I pointed to where the bridle path emerged from behind the trees—"he either saw you up here or waited until he did see you up here, and then he rode on along that stretch, giving you the usual salute by lifting his crop. But the second he got out of sight at the other end of the stretch he acted fast. He got off the horse and just left it there, knowing it would make its way back to its own exit from the park, and he beat it in a hurry, either to a Fifth Avenue bus or the subway, depending on where he was headed for. The idea was to turn the alibi on as soon as possible, since he couldn't be sure how soon the horse would be seen and the search for Keyes would be started. But at the worst he had established Keyes as still alive at ten minutes past seven, down here on the stretch, and the body would be found way uptown."

"I believe," Hefferan said stiffly, "I am on record as saying I saw Keyes."

"Scratch it," I urged him. "Blot it out. Make your mind a blank, which shouldn't—" I bit if off, deciding it would be undiplomatic, and glanced at my wrist. "It's nine minutes past seven. Where were you that morning, on your horse or off?"

"On."

"Then you'd better mount, to have it the same. Let's be particular—jump on! There he comes!"

I admit the Cossack knew how to get on top of a horse. He was erect in the saddle quicker than I would have had a foot in a stirrup, and had his gaze directed at the end of the stretch on the bridle path where it came out of the trees. I also admit the chestnut horse looked fine from up there. It was rangy but not gangly, with a proud curve to its neck, and, as Hefferan had said, it had a good set of springs. I strained my eyes to take in the details of the rider's face, but at that distance it couldn't be done. The blue of the jacket, yes, and the yellow of the breeches, and the hunched shoulders, but not the face.

No sound came from Hefferan. As the rider on the bridle path neared the end of the open stretch I strained my eyes again, hoping something would happen, knowing as I did what he would find confronting him when he rounded the sharp bend at the finish of the stretch—namely, four mounted cops abreast.

Something happened all right, fast, and not on my list of expectations. The chestnut was out of sight around the bend not more than half a second, and then here he came back, on the jump, the curve gone out of his neck. But he or his rider had had enough of the bridle path. Ten strides this side of the bend the horse swerved sharp and darted off to the left, off onto the grass in one beautiful leap, and then dead ahead, due east toward Fifth Avenue, showing us his tail. Simultaneously here came the quartet of mounted cops, like a cavalry charge. When they saw what the chestnut had done their horses' legs suddenly went stiff, slid ten feet in the loose dirt, and then sashayed for the bound onto the grass, to follow.

Yells were coming from a small mob that had run out of the forest which hid the tool shed. And Hefferan left me. His horse's ham jostled my shoulder as it sprang into action, and divots of turf flew through the air as it bounded down the slope to join the chase. The sound of gunshots came from the east, and that finished me. I would have given a year's pay, anything up to a kingdom, for a horse, but, having none, I lit out anyway.

Down the slope to the bridle path I broke records, but on the other side it was upgrade, and also I had to dodge trees and bushes and jump railings. I was making no detours to find crossings, but heading on a bee-line for the noises coming from the east, including another round of shots. One funny thing, even busy as I was trying to cover ground, I was hoping they wouldn't hit that chestnut horse. Finally the border of the park was in sight, but I could see nothing moving, though the noises seemed to be louder and closer. Straight ahead was the stone wall enclosing the park, and, unsure which way to turn for the nearest entrance, I made for the wall, climbed it, stood panting, and surveyed.

I was at Sixty-fifth and Fifth Avenue. One block up, outside a park entrance, the avenue was so cluttered that it was blocked. Cars, mostly taxis, were collecting at both fringes of the intersection, and the pedestrians who hadn't already arrived were on their way, from all directions. A bus had stopped and passengers were piling out. The tallest things there were the horses. I got the impression that there were a hell of a lot of horses, but probably it wasn't more than six or seven. They were all bays but one, the chestnut, and I was glad to see that it looked healthy as I cantered up the pavement toward the throng. The chestnut's saddle was empty.

I was pushing my way through to the center when one in uniform grabbed my arm, and I'll be damned if Officer Hefferan didn't sing out, "Let him come, that's Nero Wolfe's man Goodwin!" I would have been glad to thank him cordially, but didn't have enough breath yet to speak. So I merely pushed on and, using only my eyes, got my curiosity satisfied.

Victor Talbott, in blue jacket and yellow breeches, apparently as unhurt as the chestnut, was standing there with a city employee hanging onto each arm. His face was dirty and he looked very tired.

XV

"You will be glad to know," I told Wolfe late that afternoon, "that none of these bills we are sending to our clients will have to be addressed care of the county jail. That would be embarrassing."

It was a little after six, and he was down from the plant rooms and had beer in front of him. I was at my typewriter, making out the bills.

"Broadyke," I went on, "claims that he merely bought designs that were offered him, not knowing where they came from, and he can probably make it stick. Dorothy has agreed on a settlement with Pohl and will press no charge. As for Dorothy, it's hers now anyway, as you said, so what the hell. And Safford and Audrey can't be prosecuted just for going to ride in the park, even if they omitted it in their statements just to avoid complications. By the way, if you wonder why they allocated fifteen per cent of our fee to a stable hand, he is not a stable hand. He owns that riding academy, by gum, so Audrey hasn't sold out cheap at all—anything but. They'll probably be married on horseback."

Wolfe grunted. "That won't improve their chances any."

"You're prejudiced about marriage," I reproached him. "I may try it myself someday. Look at Saul, staked down like a tent but absolutely happy. Speaking of Saul, why did you waste money having him and Orrie phoning and calling on New York tailors?"

"It wasn't wasted," Wolfe snapped. He can't stand being accused of wasting money. "There was a slim chance that Mr. Talbott had been ass enough to have his costume made right here. The better chance, of course, was one of the cities he had recently visited, and the best of all was the one farthest away. So I telephoned Los Angeles first, and the Southwest Agency put five men on it. Also Saul and Orrie did other things. Saul learned, for instance, that Mr. Talbott's room at the hotel was so situated that, by using stairs and a side entrance, he could easily have left and returned at that time of day without being recognized." Wolfe snorted. "I doubt if Mr. Cramer even considered that. Why should he? He had taken that policeman's word that he had seen Mr. Keyes on a horse, alive and well, at ten minutes past seven."

"Good here," I agreed. "But, assuming that it might have been the murderer, not Keyes, the cop had seen alive on a horse, why did you immediately pick Talbott for it?"

"I didn't. The facts did. The masquerade, if there was one, could have helped no one but Mr. Talbott, since an alibi for that moment at that spot would have been useless for any of the others. Also the greeting exchanged at a distance with the policeman was an essential of the plan, and only Mr. Talbott, who often rode with Mr. Keyes, could have known there would be an opportunity for it."

"Okay," I conceded. "And you phoned Pohl to find out where Talbott had been recently. My God, Pohl actually helped on it! By the way, the Southwest Agency put an airmail stamp on the envelope containing their bill, so I guess they want a check. Their part of the charge is reasonable enough, but that tailor wants three hundred bucks for making a blue jacket and a pair of yellow breeches."

"Which our clients will pay," Wolfe said placidly. "It isn't exorbitant. It was five o'clock in the afternoon there when they found him, and he had to be persuaded to spend the night at it, duplicating the previous order."

"Okay," I conceded again. "I admit it had to be a real duplicate, label and all, to panic that baby. He had nerve. He gets his six-o'clock call at his hotel, says to wake him again at seven-thirty, beats it to the street without being seen, puts on his act, and gets back to his room in time to take the seven-thirty call. And don't forget he was committed right from the beginning, at half-past six, when he shot Keyes. From there on he had to make his schedule. Some nerve."

I got up and handed the bills, including copies of the itemized expense account, across to Wolfe for his inspection.

"You know," I remarked, sitting down again, "that was close to the top for a shock to the nervous system, up there this morning. When he got picked to double for Keyes that must have unsettled him a little to begin with. Then he gets ushered into the other room to change, and is handed a box that has on it 'Cleever of Hollywood.' He opens it, and there is an outfit exactly like the one he had had made, and had got well rid of somehow along with the gun, and there again is a label in the jacket, 'Cleever of Hollywood.' I'm surprised he was able to get it on and buttoned up, and walk out to the horse and climb into the saddle. He did have nerve. I suppose he intended just to keep on going, but as he rounded the bend there were the four mounted cops and flup went his nerves, and I don't blame him. I admit I hadn't the faintest idea, when I was phoning you that list of towns Pohl had given me—hey! Good God!"

Wolfe looked up. "What's the matter?"

"Give me back that expense list! I left out the ninety-five cents for Pohl's sandwiches!"

Disguise
for Murder

I

What I felt like doing was go out for a walk, but I wasn't quite desperate enough for that, so I merely beat it down to the office, shutting the door from the hall behind me, went and sat at my desk with my feet up, leaned back and closed my eyes, and took some deep breaths.

I had made two mistakes. When Bill McNab, garden editor of the *Gazette*, had suggested to Nero Wolfe that the members of the Manhattan Flower Club be invited to drop in some afternoon to look at the orchids, I should have fought it. And when the date had been set and the invitations sent, and Wolfe had arranged that Fritz and Saul should do the receiving at the front door and I should stay up in the plant rooms with him and Theodore, mingling with the guests, if I had had an ounce of brains I would have put my foot down. But I hadn't, and as a result I had been up there a good hour and a half, grinning around and acting pleased and happy. "No, sir, that's not a brasso, it's a laelio." "No, madam, I doubt if you could grow that miltonia in a living room—so sorry." "Quite all right,

madam—your sleeve happened to hook it—it'll bloom
again next year."

It wouldn't have been so bad if there had been
something for the eyes. It was understood that the
Manhattan Flower Club was choosy about who it took
in, but obviously its standards were totally different
from mine. The men were just men, okay as men go,
but the women! It was a darned good thing they had
picked on flowers to love, because flowers don't have to
love back. I didn't object to their being alive and well,
since after all I've got a mother too, and three aunts,
and I fully appreciate them, but it would have been a
relief to spot just one who could have made my grin
start farther down than the front of my teeth.

There had in fact been one—just one. I had got a
glimpse of her at the other end of the crowded aisle as
I went through the door from the cool room into the
moderate room, after showing a couple of guys what a
bale of osmundine looked like in the potting room.
From ten paces off she looked absolutely promising,
and when I had maneuvered close enough to make her
an offer to answer questions if she had any, there was
simply no doubt about it, and the first quick slanting
glance she gave me said plainly that she could tell the
difference between a flower and a man, but she just
smiled and shook her head and moved on by with her
companions, an older female and two males. Later I
had made another try and got another brushoff, and
still later, too long later, feeling that the damn grin
might freeze on me for good if I didn't take a recess, I
had gone AWOL by worming my way through to the
far end of the warm room and sidling on out.

All the way down the three flights of stairs new
guests were coming up, though it was then four
o'clock. Nero Wolfe's old brownstone house on West

Thirty-fifth Street had seen no such throng as that within my memory, which is long and good. One flight down I stopped off at my bedroom for a pack of cigarettes, and another flight down I detoured to make sure the door of Wolfe's bedroom was locked. In the main hall downstairs I halted a moment to watch Fritz Brenner, busy at the door with both departures and arrivals, and to see Paul Panzer emerge from the front room, which was being used as a cloakroom, with someone's hat and top-coat. Then, as aforesaid, I entered the office, shutting the door from the hall behind me, went and sat at my desk with my feet up, leaned back and closed my eyes, and took some deep breaths.

I had been there eight or ten minutes, and getting relaxed and a little less bitter, when the door opened and she came in. Her companions were not along. By the time she had closed the door and turned to me I had got to my feet, with a friendly leer, and had begun, "I was just sitting here thinking—"

The look on her face stopped me. There was nothing wrong with it basically, but something had got it out of kilter. She headed for me, got halfway, jerked to a stop, sank into one of the yellow chairs, and squeaked, "Could I have a drink?"

Upstairs her voice had not squeaked at all. I had liked it.

"Scotch?" I asked her. "Rye, bourbon, gin—"

She just fluttered a hand. I went to the cupboard and got a hooker of Old Woody. Her hand was shaking as she took the glass, but she didn't spill any, and she got it down in two swallows, as if it had been milk, which wasn't very ladylike. She shuddered all over and shut her eyes. In a minute she opened them again and said hoarsely, the squeak gone, "Did I need that!"

"More?"

She shook her head. Her bright brown eyes were moist, from the whisky, as she gave me a full straight look with her head tilted up. "You're Archie Goodwin," she stated.

I nodded. "And you're the Queen of Egypt?"

"I'm a baboon," she declared. "I don't know how they ever taught me to talk." She looked around for something to put the glass on, and I moved a step and reached for it. "Look at my hand shake," she complained. "I'm all to pieces."

She kept her hand out, looking at it, so I took it in mine and gave it some friendly but gentle pressure. "You do seem a little upset," I conceded. "I doubt if your hand usually feels clammy. When I saw you upstairs—"

She jerked the hand away and blurted, "I want to see Nero Wolfe. I want to see him right away, before I change my mind." She was gazing up at me, with the moist brown eyes. "My God, I'm in a fix now all right! I'm one scared baboon! I've made up my mind, I'm going to get Nero Wolfe to get me out of this somehow —why shouldn't he? He did a job for Dazy Perrit, didn't he? Then I'm through. I'll get a job at Macy's or marry a truck driver! I want to see Nero Wolfe!"

I told her it couldn't be done until the party was over.

She looked around. "Are people coming in here?"

I told her no.

"May I have another drink, please?"

I told her she should give the first one time to settle, and instead of arguing she arose and got the glass from the corner of Wolfe's desk, went to the cupboard, and helped herself. I sat down and frowned at her. Her line sounded fairly screwy for a member of the Manhattan Flower Club, or even for a daughter of one. She came back to her chair, sat, and met my eyes. Looking at her straight like that could have been a nice way to pass the time if there had been any chance for a meeting of minds, but it was easy to see that what her mind was fighting with was connected with me only accidentally.

"I could tell you," she said, hoarse again.

"Many people have," I said modestly.

"I'm going to."

"Good. Shoot."

"I'm afraid I'll change my mind and I don't want to."

"Okay. Ready, go."

"I'm a crook."

"It doesn't show," I objected. "What do you do, cheat at canasta?"

"I didn't say I'm a cheat." She cleared her throat for the hoarseness. "I said I'm a crook. Remind me someday to tell you the story of my life, how my husband got killed in the war and I broke through the gate. Don't I sound interesting?"

"You sure do. What's your line, orchid-stealing?"

"No. I wouldn't be small and I wouldn't be dirty—that's what I thought, but once you start it's not so easy. You meet people and you get involved. You can't go it alone. Two years ago four of us took over a hundred grand from a certain rich woman with a rich husband. I can tell you about that one, even names, because she couldn't move anyhow."

I nodded. "Blackmailers' customers seldom can. What—"

"I'm not a blackmailer!" Her eyes were blazing.

"Excuse me. Mr. Wolfe often says I jump to conclusions."

"You did that time." She was still indignant. "A

blackmailer's not a crook, he's a snake! Not that it really matters. What's wrong with being a crook is the other crooks—they make it dirty whether you like it or not. I've been up to my knees in it. It makes a coward of you too—that's the worst. I had a friend once—as close as a crook ever comes to having a friend—and a man killed her, strangled her, and if I had told what I knew about it they could have caught him, but I was afraid to go to the cops, so he's still loose. And she was my friend! That's getting down toward the bottom. Isn't it?"

"Fairly low," I agreed, eyeing her. "Of course I don't know you any too well. I don't know how you react to two stiff drinks. Maybe your hobby is stringing private detectives. If so, why don't you wait for Mr. Wolfe? It would be more fun with two of us."

She simply ignored it. "I realized long ago," she went on as if it were a one-way conversation, "that I had made a mistake. I wasn't what I had thought I was going to be—a romantic reckless outlaw. You can't do it that way, or anyhow I couldn't. I was just a crook and I knew it, and about a year ago I decided to break loose. A good way to do it would have been to talk to someone the way I'm talking to you now, but I didn't have sense enough to see that. And so many people were involved. It was so involved! You know?"

I nodded. "Yeah, I know."

"So I kept putting it off. We got a good one in December and I went to Florida for a vacation, but down there I met a man with a lead and we followed it up here just a week ago. That's what I'm working on now. That's what brought me here today. This man—"

She stopped abruptly.

"Well?" I invited her.

She looked dead serious, not more serious, but a

different kind. "I'm not putting anything on him," she declared. "I don't owe him anything and I don't like him, but this is strictly about me and no one else—only I had to explain why I'm here. I wish to God I'd never come!"

There was no question about that coming from her heart, unless she had done a lot of rehearsing in front of a mirror.

"It got you this talk with me," I reminded her.

She was looking straight through me and beyond. "If only I hadn't come! If only I hadn't seen him!" She leaned toward me for emphasis. "I'm either too smart or not smart enough, that's my trouble. I should have looked away from him, turned away quick, when I realized I knew who he was, before he turned and saw it in my eyes. But I was so shocked I couldn't help it! For a second I couldn't move. God, I was dumb! I stood there staring at him, thinking I wouldn't have recognized him if he hadn't had a hat on, and then he looked at me and saw what was happening. I knew then all right what an awful fool I was, and I turned away and moved off, but it was too late. I know how to manage my face with nearly anybody, anywhere, but that was too much for me. It showed so plain that Mrs. Orwin asked me what was the matter with me and I had to try to pull myself together—then seeing Nero Wolfe gave me the idea of telling him, only of course I couldn't right there with the crowd—and then I saw you going out and as soon as I could break away I came down to find you."

She tried smiling at me, but it didn't work so good. "Now I feel some better," she said hopefully.

I nodded. "That's good bourbon. Is it a secret who you recognized?"

"No. I'm going to tell Nero Wolfe."

"You decided to tell me." I flipped a hand. "Suit yourself. Whoever you tell, what good will that do?"

"Why—then he can't do anything to me."

"Why not?"

"Because he wouldn't dare. Nero Wolfe will tell him that I've told about him, so that if anything happened to me he would know it was him, and he'd know who he is—I mean Nero Wolfe would know—and so would you."

"We would if we had his name and address." I was studying her. "He must be quite a specimen, to scare you that bad. And speaking of names, what's yours?"

She made a little noise that could have been meant for a laugh. "Do you like Marjorie?"

"So-so."

"I used Evelyn Carter in Paris once. Do you like that?"

"Not bad. What are you using now?"

She hesitated, frowning.

"Good Lord," I protested, "you're not in a vacuum, and I'm a detective. They took the names down at the door."

"Cynthia Brown," she said.

"I like that fine. That's Mrs. Orwin you came with?"

"Yes."

"She's the current customer? The lead you picked up in Florida?"

"Yes. But that's—" She gestured. "That's finished. That's settled now, since I'm telling you and Nero Wolfe. I'm through."

"I know. A job at Macy's or marry a truck driver. There's one thing you haven't told me, though—who was it you recognized?"

She turned her head for a glance at the door and then turned it still farther to look behind her. When

her face came back to me it was out of kilter again,
with the teeth pinching the lower lip.

"Can anyone hear us?" she asked.

"Nope. That other door goes to the front room—
today the cloakroom. Anyhow this room's soundproofed, including the doors."

She glanced at the hall door again, returned to me,
and lowered her voice. "This has to be done the way I
say."

"Sure, why not?"

"I wasn't being honest with you."

"I wouldn't expect it from a crook. Start over."

"I mean—" She used the teeth on the lip again. "I
mean I'm not just scared about myself. I'm scared all
right, but I don't just want Nero Wolfe for what I said.
I want him to get him for murder, but he has to keep
me out of it. I don't want to have anything to do with
any cops—not now I don't especially. I'm through. If
he won't do it that way—do you think he will?"

I was feeling a faint tingle at the base of my spine. I
only get that on special occasions, but this was unquestionably something special, if Marjorie Evelyn Carter
Cynthia Brown wasn't taking me for a ride to pay for
the drinks.

I gave her a hard look and didn't let the tingle get
into my voice. "He might, for you, if you pay him. What
kind of evidence have you got? Any?"

"I saw him."

"You mean today?"

"I mean I saw him then." She had her hands
clasped tight. "I told you—I had a friend. I stopped in
at her apartment that afternoon. I was just leaving—
Doris was inside, in the bathroom—and as I got near
the entrance door I heard a key turning in the lock,
from the outside. I stopped, and the door came open

and a man came in. When he saw me he just stood and stared. I had never met Doris's bank account and I knew she didn't want me to, and since he had a key I supposed of course it was him, making an unexpected call, so I mumbled something about Doris being in the bathroom and went past him, through the door and on out."

She paused. Her clasped hands loosened and then tightened again.

"I'm burning my bridges," she said, "but I can deny all this if I have to. I went and kept a cocktail date, and then phoned Doris's number to ask if our dinner date was still on, considering the visit of the bank account. There was no answer, so I went back to her apartment and rang the bell, and there was no answer to that either. It was a self-service elevator place, no doorman or hallman, so there was no one to ask anything. Her maid found her body the next morning. The papers said she had been killed the day before. That man killed her. There wasn't a word about him—no one had seen him enter or leave. And I didn't open my mouth! I was a lousy coward!"

"And today all of a sudden there he is, looking at orchids?"

"Yes."

"It's a pretty good script," I acknowledged. "Are you sure—"

"It's no script! I wish to God it was!"

"Okay. Are you sure he knows you recognized him?"

"Yes. He looked straight at me, and his eyes—"

She was stopped by the house phone buzzing. Stepping to my desk, I picked it up and asked it, "Well?"

Nero Wolfe's voice, peevish, came. "Archie!"

"Yes, sir."

"What the devil are you doing? Come back up here!"

"Pretty soon. I'm talking with a prospective client—"

"This is no time for clients! Come at once!"

The connection went. He had slammed it down. I hung up and went back to the prospective client. "Mr. Wolfe wants me upstairs. He didn't stop to think in time that the Manhattan Flower Club has women in it as well as men. Do you want to wait here?"

"Yes."

"If Mrs. Orwin asks about you?"

"I didn't feel well and went home."

"Okay. I shouldn't be long—the invitations said two-thirty to five. If you want a drink, help yourself. What name does this murderer use when he goes to look at orchids?"

She looked blank. I got impatient.

"Damn it, what's his name? This bird you recognized."

"I don't know."

"You don't?"

"No."

"Describe him."

She thought it over a little, gazing at me, and then shook her head. "I don't think—" she said doubtfully. She shook her head again, more positive. "Not now. I want to see what Nero Wolfe says first." She must have seen something in my eyes, or thought she did, for suddenly she came up out of her chair and moved to me and put a hand on my arm. "That's all I mean," she said earnestly. "It's not you—I know you're all right." Her fingers tightened on my forearm. "I might as well tell you—you'd never want any part of me anyhow— this is the first time in years, I don't know how long, that I've talked to a man just straight—you know, just human? You know, not figuring on something one way or another. I—" She stopped for a word, and a little color showed in her cheeks. She found the word. "I've enjoyed it very much."

"Good. Me too. Call me Archie. I've got to go, but describe him. Just sketch him."

But she hadn't enjoyed it that much. "Not until Nero Wolfe says he'll do it," she said firmly.

I had to leave it at that, knowing as I did that in three more minutes Wolfe might have a fit. Out in the hall I had the notion of passing the word to Saul and Fritz to give departing guests a good look, but rejected it because (a) they weren't there, both of them presumably being busy in the cloakroom, (b) he might have departed already, and (c) I had by no means swallowed a single word of Cynthia's story, let alone the whole works. So I headed for the stairs and breasted the descending tide of guests leaving.

Up in the plant rooms there were plenty left. When I came into Wolfe's range he darted me a glance of cold fury, and I turned on the grin. Anyway, it was a quarter to five, and if they took the hint on the invitation it wouldn't last much longer.

II

They didn't take the hint on the dot, but it didn't bother me because my mind was occupied. I was now really interested in them—or at least one of them, if he had actually been there and hadn't gone home.

First there was a chore to get done. I found the three Cynthia had been with, a female and two males, over by the odontoglossum bench in the cool room.

Getting through to them, I asked politely, "Mrs. Orwin?"

She nodded at me and said, "Yes?" Not quite tall enough but plenty plump enough, with a round full face and narrow little eyes that might have been better if they had been wide open, she struck me as a lead worth following. Just the pearls around her neck and the mink stole over her arm would have made a good haul, though I doubted if that was the kind of loot Cynthia specialized in.

"I'm Archie Goodwin," I said. "I work here."

I would have gone on if I had known how, but I needed a lead myself, since I didn't know whether to say Miss Brown or Mrs. Brown. Luckily one of the males horned in.

"My sister?" he inquired anxiously.

So it was a brother-and-sister act. As far as looks went he wasn't a bad brother at all. Older than me maybe, but not much, he was tall and straight, with a strong mouth and jaw and keen gray eyes. "My sister?" he repeated.

"I guess so. You are—"

"Colonel Brown. Percy Brown."

"Yeah." I switched back to Mrs. Orwin. "Miss Brown asked me to tell you that she went home. I gave her a little drink and it seemed to help, but she decided to leave. She asked me to apologize for her."

"She's perfectly healthy," the colonel asserted. He sounded a little hurt. "There's nothing wrong with her."

"Is she all right?" Mrs. Orwin asked.

"For her," the other male put in, "you should have made it three drinks. Three big ones. Or just hand her the bottle."

His tone was mean and his face was mean, and any-

how that was no way to talk in front of the help in a
strange house, meaning me. He was some younger
than Colonel Brown, but he already looked enough like
Mrs. Orwin, especially the eyes, to make it more than a
guess that they were mother and son. That point was
settled when she commanded him, "Be quiet, Gene!"
She turned to the colonel. "Perhaps you should go and
see about her?"

He shook his head, with a fond but manly smile at
her. "It's not necessary, Mimi. Really."

"She's all right," I assured them and pushed off,
thinking there were a lot of names in this world that
could stand a reshuffle. Calling that overweight nar-
row-eyed pearl-and-mink proprietor Mimi was a para-
dox.

I moved around among the guests, being gracious.
Fully aware that I was not equipped with a Geiger
counter that would flash a signal if and when I established a contact with a strangler, the fact remained
that I had been known to have hunches, and it would
be something for my scrapbook if I picked one as the
killer of Doris Hatten and it turned out later to be
sunfast.

Cynthia Brown hadn't given me the Hatten, only
the Doris, but with the context that was enough. At
the time it had happened, some five months ago, early
in October, the papers had given it a big play of course.
She had been strangled with her own scarf, of white
silk with the Declaration of Independence printed on
it, in her cozy fifth-floor apartment in the West Seven-
ties, and the scarf had been left around her neck, knot-
ted at the back. The cops had never got within a mile
of charging anyone, and Sergeant Purley Stebbins of
Homicide had told me that they had never even found

out who was paying the rent, but there was no law against Purley being discreet.

I kept on the go through the plant rooms, leaving all switches open for a hunch. Some of them were plainly preposterous, but with everyone else I made an opportunity to exchange some words, fullface and close up. That took time, and it was no help to my current and chronic campaign for a raise in wages, since it was the women, not the men, that Wolfe wanted off his neck. I stuck at it anyhow. It was true that if Cynthia was on the level, and if she hadn't changed her mind by the time I got Wolfe in to her, we would soon have specifications, but I had had that tingle at the bottom of my spine and I was stubborn.

As I say, it took time, and meanwhile five o'clock came and went, and the crowd thinned out. Going on five-thirty the remaining groups seemed to get the idea all at once that time was up and made for the entrance to the stairs. I was in the moderate room when it happened, and the first thing I knew I was alone there, except for a guy at the north bench, studying a row of dowianas. He didn't interest me, as I had already canvassed him and crossed him off as the wrong type for a strangler, but as I glanced his way he suddenly bent forward to pick up a pot with a flowering plant, and as he did so I felt my back stiffening. The stiffening was a reflex, but I knew what had caused it: the way his fingers closed around the pot, especially the thumbs. No matter how careful you are of other people's property, you don't pick up a five-inch pot as if you were going to squeeze the life out of it.

I made my way around to him. When I got there he was holding the pot so that the flowers were only a few inches from his eyes.

"Nice flower," I said brightly.

He nodded. "What color do you call the sepals?"

"Nankeen yellow."

He leaned to put the pot back, still choking it. I swiveled my head. The only people in sight, beyond the glass partition between us and the cool room, were Nero Wolfe and a small group of guests, among whom were the Orwin trio and Bill McNab, the garden editor of the *Gazette*. As I turned my head back to my man he straightened up, pivoted on his heel, and marched off without a word. Whatever else he might or might not have been guilty of, he certainly had bad manners.

I followed him, on into the warm room and through, out to the landing, and down the three flights of stairs. Along the main hall I was courteous enough not to step on his heel, but a lengthened stride would have reached it. The hall was next to empty. A woman, ready for the street in a caracul coat, was standing there, and Saul Panzer was posted near the front door with nothing to do. I followed my man on into the front room, the cloakroom, where Fritz Brenner was helping a guest on with his coat. Of course the racks were practically bare, and with one glance my man saw his property and went to get it. His coat was a brown tweed that had been through a lot more than one winter. I stepped forward to help, but he ignored me without even bothering to shake his head. I was beginning to feel hurt. When he emerged to the hall I was beside him, and as he moved to the front door I spoke.

"Excuse me, but we're checking guests out as well as in. Your name, please?"

"Ridiculous," he said curtly, and reached for the knob, pulled the door open, and crossed the sill. Saul, knowing I must have had a reason for wanting to check him out, was at my elbow, and we stood watching his back as he descended the seven steps of the stoop.

"Tail?" Saul muttered at me.

I shook my head and was parting my lips to mutter something back, when a sound came from behind us that made us both whirl around—a screech from a woman, not loud but full of feeling. As we whirled, Fritz and the guest he had been serving came out of the front room, and all four of us saw the woman in the caracul coat come running out of the office into the hall. She kept coming, gasping something, and the guest, making a noise like an alarmed male, moved to meet her. I moved faster, needing about eight jumps to the office door and two inside. There I stopped.

Of course I knew the thing on the floor was Cynthia, but only because I had left her in there in those clothes. With the face blue and contorted, the tongue halfway out, and the eyes popping, it could have been almost anybody. I knelt and slipped my hand inside her dress front, kept it there ten seconds, and felt nothing.

Saul's voice came from behind. "I'm here."

I got up and went to the phone on my desk and started dialing, telling Saul, "No one leaves. We'll keep what we've got. Have the door open for Doc Vollmer." After only two whirs the nurse answered, and put Vollmer on, and I snapped it at him. "Doc, Archie Goodwin. Come on the run. Strangled woman. Yeah, strangled."

I pushed the phone back, reached for the house phone and buzzed the plant rooms, and after a wait had Wolfe's irritated bark in my ear. "Yes?"

"I'm in the office. You'd better come down. That prospective client I mentioned is here on the floor, strangled. I think she's gone, but I've sent for Vollmer."

"Is this flummery?" he roared.

"No, sir. Come down and look at her and then ask me."

The connection went. He had slammed it down. I got a sheet of thin tissue paper from a drawer, tore off a corner, and went and placed it carefully over Cynthia's mouth and nostrils. In ten seconds it hadn't stirred.

Voices had been sounding from the hall. Now one of them entered the office. Its owner was the guest who had been in the cloakroom with Fritz when the screech came. He was a chunky broad-shouldered guy with sharp domineering dark eyes and arms like a gorilla's. His voice was going strong as he started toward me from the door, but it stopped when he had come far enough to get a good look at the object on the floor.

"My God," he said huskily.

"Yes, sir," I agreed.

"How did it happen?"

"Don't know."

"Who is it?"

"Don't know."

He made his eyes come away from it and up until they met mine, and I gave him an A for control. It really was a sight.

"The man at the door won't let us leave," he stated.

"No, sir. You can see why."

"I certainly can." His eyes stayed with me, however. "But we know nothing about it. My name is Carlisle, Homer N. Carlisle. I am the executive vice-president of the North American Foods Company. My wife was merely acting under impulse; she wanted to see the office of Nero Wolfe, and she opened the door and entered. She's sorry she did, and so am I. We have an appointment, and there's no reason why we should be detained."

"I'm sorry too," I told him. "But one thing, if nothing else—your wife discovered the body. We're stuck worse than you are, with a corpse here in our office, and we haven't even got a wife who had an impulse. We got it for nothing. So I guess— Hello, Doc."

Vollmer, entering and nodding at me on the fly, was panting a little as he set his black case on the floor and knelt beside it. His house was down the street and he had had only two hundred yards to trot, but he was taking on weight. As he opened the case and got out the stethoscope, Homer Carlisle stood and watched with his lips pressed tight, and I did likewise until I heard the sound of Wolfe's elevator. Crossing to the door and into the hall, I surveyed the terrain. Toward the front Saul and Fritz were calming down the woman in the caracul coat, now Mrs. Carlisle to me. Nero Wolfe and Mrs. Mimi Orwin were emerging from the elevator. Four guests were coming down the stairs: Gene Orwin, Colonel Percy Brown, Bill McNab, and a middle-aged male with a mop of black hair.

I stayed by the office door to block the quartet on the stairs. As Wolfe headed for me, Mrs. Carlisle darted to him and grabbed his arm. "I only wanted to see your office! I want to go! I'm not—"

As she pulled at him and sputtered, I noted a detail. The caracul coat was unfastened, and the ends of a silk scarf, figured and gaily colored, were flying loose. Since at least half of the female guests had sported scarfs, I mention it only to be honest and admit that I had got touchy on that subject.

Wolfe, who had already been too close to too many women that day to suit him, tried to jerk away, but she hung on. She was the big-boned flat-chested athletic type, and it could have been quite a tussle, with him weighing twice as much as her and four times as big

around, if Saul hadn't rescued him by coming in between and prying her loose. That didn't stop her
tongue, but Wolfe ignored it and came on toward me.

"Has Dr. Vollmer come?"

"Yes, sir."

The executive vice-president emerged from the office, talking. "Mr. Wolfe, my name is Homer N. Carlisle
and I insist—"

"Shut up," Wolfe growled. On the sill of the door to
the office, he faced the audience. "Flower lovers," he
said with bitter scorn. "You told me, Mr. McNab, a
distinguished group of sincere and devoted gardeners.
Pfui! Saul!"

"Yes, sir."

"Are you armed?"

"Yes, sir."

"Put them all in the dining room and keep them
there. Let no one touch anything around this door, especially the knob. Archie, come with me."

He wheeled and entered the office. Following, I
used my foot to swing the door nearly shut, leaving no
crack but not latching it. When I turned Vollmer was
standing, facing Wolfe's scowl.

"Well?" Wolfe demanded.

"Dead," Vollmer told him. "With asphyxiation from
strangling sometimes you can do something, but it
wasn't even worth trying."

"How long ago?"

"I don't know, but not more than an hour or two.
Two hours at the outside, probably less."

Wolfe looked at the thing on the floor, with no
change in his scowl, and back at Doc. "You say strangling. Finger marks?"

"No. A constricting band of something with pressure below the hyoid bone. Not a stiff or narrow band; something soft like a strip of cloth—say a scarf."

Wolfe switched to me. "You didn't notify the police."

"No, sir." I glanced at Vollmer and back. "I need a word."

"I suppose so." He spoke to Doc. "If you will leave us for a moment? The front room?"

Vollmer hesitated, uncomfortable. "As a doctor called to a violent death I'd catch hell. Of course I could say—"

"Then go to a corner and cover your ears."

He did so. He went to the farthest corner, the angle made by the partition of the bathroom, pressed his palms to his ears, and stood facing us.

I addressed Wolfe with a lowered voice. "I was here, and she came in. She was either scared good or putting on a very fine act. Apparently it wasn't an act, and I now think I should have alerted Saul and Fritz, but it doesn't matter what I now think. Last October a woman named Doris Hatten was killed—strangled—in her apartment. No one got elected. Remember?"

"Yes."

"She said she was a friend of Doris Hatten's and was at her apartment that day and saw the man that did the strangling, and that he was here this afternoon. She said he was aware that she had recognized him, that's why she was scared, and she wanted to get you to help by telling him that we were wise and he'd better lay off. No wonder I didn't gulp it down. I realize that you dislike complications and therefore might want to scratch this out, but at the end she touched a soft spot by saying that she had enjoyed my company, so I prefer to open up to the cops."

"Then do so. Confound it!"

I went to the phone and started dialing WAtkins 9-8241. Doc Vollmer came out of his corner and went to get his black case from the floor and put it on a chair. Wolfe was pathetic. He moved around behind his desk and lowered himself into his own oversized custom-made number, the only spot on earth where he was ever completely comfortable, but there smack in front of him was the object on the floor, so after a moment he made a face, got back onto his feet, grunted like an outraged boar, went across to the other side of the room to the shelves, and inspected the backbones of books.

But even that pitiful diversion got interrupted. As I finished with my phone call and hung up, sudden sounds of commotion came from the hall. Dashing across, getting fingernails on the edge of the door and pulling it open, and passing through, I saw trouble. A group was gathered in the open doorway of the dining room, which was across the hall. Saul Panzer went bounding past me toward the front. At the front door Colonel Percy Brown was stiff-arming Fritz Brenner with one hand and reaching for the doorknob with the other. Fritz, who is chef and housekeeper, is not supposed to double in acrobatics, but he did fine. Dropping to the floor, he grabbed the colonel's ankles and jerked his feet out from under him. Then I was there, and Saul with his gun out; and there with us was the guest with the mop of black hair.

"You damn fool," I told the colonel as he sat up. "If you'd got outdoors Saul would have winged you."

"Guilt," said the black-haired guest emphatically. "The compression got unbearable and he exploded. I was watching him. I'm a psychiatrist."

"Good for you." I took his elbow and turned him.

"Go back in and watch all of 'em. With that wall mirror you can include yourself."

"This is illegal," stated Colonel Brown, who had scrambled to his feet and was short of breath.

Saul herded them to the rear. Fritz got hold of my sleeve. "Archie, I've got to ask Mr. Wolfe about dinner."

"Nuts," I said savagely. "By dinnertime this place will be more crowded than it was this afternoon. Company is coming, sent by the city. It's a good thing we have a cloakroom ready."

"But he has to eat; you know that. I should have the ducks in the oven now. If I have to stay here at the door and attack people as they try to leave, what will he eat?"

"Nuts," I said. I patted him on the shoulder. "Excuse my manners, Fritz, I'm upset. I've just strangled a young woman."

"Nuts," he said scornfully.

"I might as well have," I declared.

The doorbell rang. I reached for the switch and turned on the stoop light and looked through the panel of one-way glass. It was the first consignment of cops.

III

In my opinion Inspector Cramer made a mistake. Opinion, hell, of course he did. It is true that in a room where a murder has occurred the city scientists—measurers, sniffers, print-takers, specialists, photographers—may shoot the works, and they do. But except in rare circumstances the job shouldn't take all week, and in the case of our office a couple of hours should have been ample. In fact, it was. By eight o'clock the

scientists were through. But Cramer, like a sap, gave
the order to seal it up until further notice, in Wolfe's
hearing. He knew damn well that Wolfe spent as least
three hundred evenings a year in there, in the only
chair and under the only light that he really liked, and
that was why he did it. It was a mistake. If he hadn't
made it, Wolfe might have called his attention to a
certain fact as soon as Wolfe saw it himself, and
Cramer would have been saved a lot of trouble.

The two of them got the fact at the same time, from
me. We were in the dining room—this was shortly after the scientists had got busy in the office, and the
guests, under guard, had been shunted to the front
room—and I was relating my conversation with
Cynthia Brown. They wanted all of it, or Cramer did
rather, and they got it. Whatever else my years as
Wolfe's assistant may have done for me or to me, they
have practically turned me into a tape recorder, and
Wolfe and Cramer didn't get a rewrite of that conversation, they got the real thing, word for word. They
also got the rest of my afternoon, complete. When I
finished, Cramer had a slew of questions, but Wolfe not
a one. Maybe he had already focused on the fact above
referred to, but neither Cramer nor I had. The shorthand dick seated at one end of the dining table had the
fact too, in his notebook along with the rest of it, but he
wasn't supposed to focus.

Cramer called a recess on the questions to take
steps. He called men in and gave orders. Colonel
Brown was to be photographed and fingerprinted and
headquarters records were to be checked for him and
Cynthia. The file on the murder of Doris Hatten was to
be brought to him at once. The lab reports were to be
rushed. Saul Panzer and Fritz Brenner were to be
brought in.

They came. Fritz stood like a soldier at attention, grim and grave. Saul, only five feet seven, with the sharpest eyes and one of the biggest noses I have ever seen, in his unpressed brown suit, and his necktie crooked—he stood like Saul, not slouching and not stiff. He would stand like that if he were being awarded the Medal of Honor or if he were in front of a firing squad.

Of course Cramer knew both of them. He picked on Saul. "You and Fritz were in the hall all afternoon?"

Saul nodded. "The hall and the front room, yes."

"Who did you see enter or leave the office?"

"I saw Archie go in about four o'clock—I was just coming out of the front room with someone's hat and coat. I saw Mrs. Carlisle come out just after she screamed. In between those two I saw no one either enter or leave. We were busy most of the time, either in the hall or the front room."

Cramer grunted. "How about you, Fritz?"

"I saw no one." Fritz spoke louder than usual. "I didn't even see Archie go in." He took a step forward, still like a soldier. "I would like to say something."

"Go ahead."

"I think a great deal of all this disturbance is unnecessary. My duties here are of the household and not professional, but I cannot help hearing what reaches my ears, and I am aware of the many times that Mr. Wolfe has found the answer to problems that were too much for you. This happened here in his own house, and I think it should be left entirely to him."

I yooped, "Fritz, I didn't know you had it in you!"

"All this disturbance," he insisted firmly.

"I'll be goddamned." Cramer was goggling at him. "Wolfe told you to say that, huh?"

"Bah." Wolfe was contemptuous. "It can't be helped, Fritz. Have we plenty of ham?"

"Yes, sir."

"Sturgeon?"

"Yes, sir."

"Later, probably. For the guests in the front room, but not the police. Are you through with them, Mr. Cramer?"

"No." Cramer went back to Saul. "You checked the guests in?"

"Yes."

"How?"

"I had a list of the members of the Manhattan Flower Club. They had to show their membership cards. I checked on the list those who came. If they brought a wife or husband, or any other guest, I took the names."

"Then you have a record of everybody?"

"Yes."

"How complete is it?"

"It's complete and it's accurate."

"About how many names?"

"Two hundred and nineteen."

"This place wouldn't hold that many."

Saul nodded. "They came and went. There wasn't more than a hundred or so at any one time."

"That's a help." Cramer was getting more and more disgusted, and I didn't blame him. "Goodwin says he was there at the door with you when that woman screamed and came running out of the office, but that you hadn't seen her enter the office. Why not?"

"We had our backs turned. We were watching a man who had just left go down the steps. Archie had asked him for his name and he had said that was ridiculous. If you want it, his name is Malcolm Vedder."

"The hell it is. How do you know?"

"I had checked him in along with the rest."

Cramer stared. "Are you telling me that you could fit that many names to that many faces after seeing them just once?"

Saul's shoulders went slightly up and down. "There's more to people than faces. I might go wrong on a few, but not many. I was at that door to do a job and I did it."

"You should know by this time," Wolfe rumbled, "that Mr. Panzer is an exceptional man."

Cramer spoke to a dick standing by the door. "You heard that name, Levy—Malcolm Vedder. Tell Stebbins to check it on that list and send a man to bring him in."

The dick went. Cramer returned to Saul. "Put it this way. Say I sit you here with that list, and a man or woman is brought in, and I point to a name on the list and ask you if that person came this afternoon under that name. Could you tell me positively?"

"I could tell you positively whether the person had been here or not, especially if he was wearing the same clothes and hadn't been disguised. On fitting him to his name I might go wrong in a few cases, but I doubt it."

"I don't believe you."

"Mr. Wolfe does," Saul said complacently. "Archie does. I have developed my faculties."

"You sure have. All right, that's all for now. Stick around."

Saul and Fritz went. Wolfe, in his own chair at the end of the dining table, where ordinarily, at this hour, he sat for a quite different purpose than the one at hand, heaved a deep sigh and closed his eyes. I, seated beside Cramer at the side of the table that put us facing the door to the hall, was beginning to appreciate

the kind of problem we were up against. The look on
Cramer's face indicated that he was appreciating it
too. The look was crossing my bow, direct at Wolfe.

"Goodwin's story," Cramer growled. "I mean her
story. What do you think?"

Wolfe's eyes came open a little. "What followed
seems to support it. I doubt if she would have arranged for that"—he flipped a hand in the direction of
the office across the hall—"just to corroborate a tale. I
accept it. I credit it."

"Yeah. I don't need to remind you that I know you
well and I know Goodwin well. So I wonder how much
chance there is that in a day or so you'll suddenly remember that she had been here before today, or one or
more of the others had, and you've got a client, and
there was something leading up to this."

"Bosh," Wolfe said dryly. "Even if it were like that,
and it isn't, you would be wasting time. Since you know
us, you know we wouldn't remember until we got
ready to."

Cramer glowered. Two scientists came in from
across the hall to report. Stebbins came to announce
the arrival of an assistant district attorney. A dick
came to relay a phone call from a deputy commissioner.
Another dick came in to say that Homer Carlisle was
raising hell in the front room. Meanwhile Wolfe sat
with his eyes shut, but I got an idea of his state of mind
from the fact that intermittently his forefinger was
making little circles on the polished top of the table.

Cramer looked at him. "What do you know," he
asked abruptly, "about the killing of that Doris Hatten?"

"Newspaper accounts," Wolfe muttered. "And
what Mr. Stebbins has told Mr. Goodwin, casually."

"Casual is right." Cramer got out a cigar, conveyed

it to his mouth, and sank his teeth in it. He never lit one. "Those damn houses with self-service elevators are worse than walk-ups for a checking job. No one ever sees anyone coming or going. If you're not interested, I'm talking to hear myself."

"I am interested." Wolfe's eyes stayed shut.

"Good. I appreciate it. Even so, self-service elevator or not, the man who paid the rent for that apartment was lucky. He may have been clever and careful, but also he was lucky. Never to have anybody see him enough to give a description of him—that took luck."

"Possibly Miss Hatten paid the rent herself."

"Sure," Cramer conceded, "she paid it all right, but where did she get it from? No visible means of support —he sure wasn't visible, and three good men spent a month trying to start a trail, and one of them is still at it. There was no doubt about its being that kind of a setup; we did get that far. She had only been living there two months, and when we found out how well the man who paid for it had kept himself covered, as tight as a drum, we decided that maybe he had installed her there just for the purpose. That was why we gave it all we had. Another reason was that the papers started hinting that we knew who he was and that he was such a big shot we were sitting on the lid."

Cramer shifted his cigar one tooth over to the left. "That kind of thing used to get me sore, but what the hell, for newspapers that's just routine. Big shot or not, he didn't need us to do any covering for him—he had done too good a job himself. Now, if we're to take it the way this Cynthia Brown gave it to Goodwin, it might have been the man who paid the rent and it might not. That makes it pie. I would hate to tell you what I think of the fact that Goodwin sat there in your office and was told right here on these premises and all

he did was go upstairs and watch to see if anybody
squeezed a flowerpot!"

"You're irritated," I said charitably. "Not that he
was on the premises, that he *had* been. Also I was
taking it with salt. Also she was saving specifications
for Mr. Wolfe. Also—"

"Also I know you. How many of those two hundred
and nineteen people were men?"

"I would say a little over half."

"Then how do *you* like it?"

"I hate it."

Wolfe grunted. "Judging from your attitude, Mr.
Cramer, something that has occurred to me has not
occurred to you."

"Naturally. You're a genius. What is it?"

"Something that Mr. Goodwin told us. I want to
consider it a little."

"We could consider it together."

"Later. Those people in the front room are my
guests. Can't you dispose of them?"

"One of your guests," Cramer rasped, "was a beaut,
all right." He spoke to the dick by the door. "Bring in
that woman—what's her name? Carlisle."

I V

Mrs. Homer N. Carlisle came in with all her belong-
ings: her caracul coat, her gaily colored scarf, and her
husband. Perhaps I should say that her husband
brought her. As soon as he was through the door he
strode across to the dining table and delivered a ha-
rangue. I don't suppose Cramer had heard that speech,
with variations, more than a thousand times. This time
it was pretty offensive. Solid and broad-shouldered,

Mr. Carlisle looked the part. His sharp dark eyes flashed, and his long gorilla-like arms were good for gestures. At the first opening Cramer, controlling himself, said he was sorry and asked them to sit down.

Mrs. Carlisle did. Mr. Carlisle didn't.

"We're nearly two hours late now," he stated. "I know you have your duty to perform, but citizens have a few rights left, thank God. Our presence here is purely adventitious." I would have been impressed by the adventitious if he hadn't had so much time to think it up. "I warn you that if my name is published in connection with this miserable affair, a murder in the house of a private detective, I'll make trouble. I'm in a position to. Why should it be? Why should we be detained? What if we had left five or ten minutes earlier, as others did?"

"That's not quite logical," Cramer objected.

"Why not?"

"No matter when you left it would have been the same if your wife had acted the same. She discovered the body."

"By accident!"

"May I say something, Homer?" the wife put in.

"It depends on what you say."

"Oh," Cramer said significantly.

"What do you mean, oh?" Carlisle demanded.

"I mean that I sent for your wife, not you, but you came with her, and that tells me why. You wanted to see to it that she wasn't indiscreet."

"What the hell has she got to be indiscreet about?"

"I don't know. Apparently you do. If she hasn't, why don't you sit down and relax while I ask her a few questions?"

"I would, sir," Wolfe advised him. "You came in

here angry, and you blundered. An angry man is a jackass."

It was a struggle for the executive vice-president, but he made it. He clamped his jaws and sat. Cramer went to the wife.

"You wanted to say something, Mrs. Carlisle?"

"Only that I'm sorry." Her bony hands, the fingers twined, were on the table before her. "For the trouble I've caused."

"I wouldn't say you caused it exactly—except for yourself and your husband." Cramer was mild. "The woman was dead, whether you went in there or not. But, if only as a matter of form, it was essential for me to see you, since you discovered the body. That's all there is to it as far as I know. There's no question of your being involved more than that."

"How the hell could there be?" Carlisle blurted.

Cramer ignored him. "Goodwin here saw you standing in the hall not more than two minutes, probably less, prior to the moment you screamed and ran out of the office. How long had you then been downstairs?"

"We had just come down. I was waiting for my husband to get his things."

"Had you been downstairs before that?"

"No—only when we came in."

"What time did you arrive?"

"A little after three, I think—"

"Twenty past three," the husband put in.

"Were you and your husband together all the time? Continuously?"

"Of course. Well—you know how it is—he would want to look longer at something, and I would move on a little—"

"Certainly we were," Carlisle said irritably. "You can see why I made that remark about it depending on

what she said. She has a habit of being vague. This is
no time to be vague."

"I am not actually vague," she protested with no
heat, not to her husband but to Cramer. "It's just that
everything is relative. There would be no presence if
there were no absence. There would be no innocence if
there were no sin. Nothing can be cut off sharp from
anything else. Who would have thought my wish to see
Nero Wolfe's office would link me with a horrible
crime?"

"My God!" Carlisle exploded. "Hear that? Link.
Link!"

"Why did you want to see Wolfe's office?" Cramer
inquired.

"Why, to see the globe."

I gawked at her. I had supposed that naturally she
would say it was curiosity about the office of a great
and famous detective. Apparently Cramer reacted the
same as me. "The globe?" he demanded.

"Yes, I had read about it and I wanted to see how it
looked. I thought a globe that size, three feet in diame-
ter, would be fantastic in an ordinary room—Oh!"

"Oh what?"

"I didn't see it!"

Cramer nodded. "You saw something else instead.
By the way, I forgot to ask, did you know her? Had
you ever seen her before?"

"You mean—her?"

"Yes. Her name was Cynthia Brown."

"We had never known her or seen her or heard of
her," the husband declared.

"Had you, Mrs. Carlisle?"

"No."

"Of course she came as the guest of a Mrs. Orwin;

she wasn't a member of this flower club. Are you a member?"

"My husband is."

"We both are," Carlisle stated. "Vague again. It's a joint membership. In my greenhouse at my country home I have over four thousand plants, including several hundred orchids." He looked at his wrist watch. "Isn't this about enough?"

"Plenty," Cramer conceded. "Thank you, both of you. We won't bother you again unless we have to. Levy, pass them out."

Mrs. Carlisle got to her feet and moved off, but halfway to the door she turned. "I don't suppose— would it be possible for me to look at the globe now? Just a peek?"

"For God's sake!" Her husband took her by the arm. "Come on. Come on!"

When the door had closed behind them Cramer glared at me and then at Wolfe. "This is sure a sweet one," he said grimly. "Say it's within the range of possibility that Carlisle is it, and the way it stands right now, why not? So we look into him. We check back on him for six months, and try doing it without getting roars out of him—a man like that, in his position. However, it can be done—by three or four men in two or three weeks. Multiply that by what? How many men were here?"

"Around a hundred and twenty," I told him. "Ten dozen. But you'll find that at least half of them are disqualified one way or another. As I told you, I took a survey. Say sixty."

"All right, multiply it by sixty. Do you care for it?"

"No."

"Neither do I." Cramer took the cigar from his mouth, removed a nearly severed piece with his fingers and put it in an ashtray, and replaced the cigar with a fresh tooth-hold. "Of course," he said sarcastically, "when she sat in there telling you about him the situation was different. You wanted her to enjoy being with you. You couldn't reach for the phone and tell us you had a self-confessed crook who could put a quick finger on a murderer and let us come and take over— hell no! You had to save it for a fee for Wolfe! You had to sit and admire her legs!"

"Don't be vulgar," I said severely.

"You had to go upstairs and make a survey! You had to— Well?"

Lieutenant Rowcliff had opened the door and entered. There were some city employees I liked, some I admired, some I had no feeling about, some I could have done without easy—and one whose ears I was going to twist someday. That was Rowcliff. He was tall, strong, handsome, and a pain in the neck.

"We're all through in there, sir," he said importantly. "We've covered everything. Nothing is being taken away, and it is all in order. We were especially careful with the contents of the drawers of Wolfe's desk, and also we—"

"My desk!" Wolfe roared.

"Yes, your desk," Rowcliff said precisely, smirking.

The blood was rushing into Wolfe's face.

"She was killed there," Cramer said gruffly. "She was strangled with something, and murderers have been known to hide things. Did you get anything at all?"

"I don't think so," Rowcliff admitted. "Of course the prints have to be sorted, and there'll be lab reports. How do we leave it?"

"Seal it up and we'll see tomorrow. You stay here

and keep a photographer. The others can go. Tell Stebbins to send that woman in—Mrs. Irwin."

"Orwin, sir."

"I'll see her."

"Yes, sir." Rowcliff turned to go.

"Wait a minute," I objected. "Seal what up? The office?"

"Certainly," Rowcliff sneered.

I said firmly, to Cramer, not to him, "You don't mean it. We work there. We live there. All our stuff is there."

"Go ahead, Lieutenant," Cramer told Rowcliff, and he wheeled and went.

I set my jaw. I was full of both feelings and words, but I knew they had to be held in. This was not for me. This was far and away the worst Cramer had ever pulled. It was up to Wolfe. I looked at him. The blood had gone back down again; he was white with fury, and his mouth was pressed to so tight a line that there were no lips.

"It's routine," Cramer said aggressively.

Wolfe said icily, "That's a lie. It is not routine."

"It's *my* routine—in a case like this. Your office is not just an office. It's the place where more fancy tricks have been played than any other spot in New York. When a woman is murdered there, soon after a talk with Goodwin for which we have no word but his, I say sealing it is routine."

Wolfe's head came forward an inch, his chin out. "No, Mr. Cramer. I'll tell you what it is. It is the malefic spite of a sullen little soul and a crabbed and envious mind. It is the childish rancor of a primacy too often challenged and offended. It is the feeble wriggle—"

The door came open to let Mrs. Orwin in.

V

With Mrs. Carlisle the husband had come along. With Mrs. Orwin it was the son. His expression and manner were so different I would hardly have known him. Upstairs his tone had been mean and his face had been mean. Now his narrow little eyes were doing their damnedest to look frank and cordial and one of the boys. He leaned across the table at Cramer, extending a hand.

"Inspector Cramer? I've been hearing about you for years! I'm Eugene Orwin." He glanced to his right. "I've already had the pleasure of meeting Mr. Wolfe and Mr. Goodwin—earlier today, before this terrible thing happened. It *is* terrible."

"Yes," Cramer agreed. "Sit down."

"I will in a moment. I do better with words standing up. I would like to make a statement on behalf of my mother and myself, and I hope you'll permit it. I'm a member of the bar. My mother is not feeling well. At the request of your men she went in with me to identify the body of Miss Brown, and it was a bad shock, and we've been detained now more than two hours."

His mother's appearance corroborated him. Sitting with her head propped on a hand and her eyes closed, obviously she didn't care as much about the impression they made on the inspector as her son did. It was doubtful whether she was paying any attention to what her son was saying.

"A statement would be welcome," Cramer told him, "if it's relevant."

"I thought so," Gene said approvingly. "So many people have an entirely wrong idea of police methods! Of course you know that Miss Brown came here today as my mother's guest, and therefore it might be supposed that my mother knows her well. But actually she doesn't. That's what I want to make clear."

"Go ahead."

Gene glanced at the shorthand dick. "If it's taken down I would like to go over it when convenient."

"You may."

"Then here are the facts. In January my mother was in Florida. You meet all kinds in Florida. My mother met a man who called himself Colonel Percy Brown—a British colonel in the Reserve, he said. Later on he introduced his sister Cynthia to her. My mother saw a great deal of them. My father is dead, and the estate, a rather large one, is in her control. She lent Brown some money—not much; that was just an opener. A week ago—"

Mrs. Orwin's head jerked up. "It was only five thousand dollars, and I didn't promise him anything," she said wearily, and propped her head on her hand again.

"All right, Mother." Gene patted her shoulder. "A week ago she returned to New York, and they came along. The first time I met them I thought they were impostors. He didn't sound like an Englishman, and certainly she didn't. They weren't very free with family details, but from them and Mother, chiefly Mother, I got enough to inquire about and sent a cable to London. I got a reply Saturday and another one this morning, and there was more than enough to confirm my suspicion, but not nearly enough to put it up to my mother. When she likes people she can be very stubborn about them—not a bad trait, not at all; I don't want to be misunderstood and I don't want her to be. I was thinking it over, what step to take next. Meanwhile, I thought it best not to let them be alone with her if I could help it—as you see, I'm being utterly frank. That's why I came here with them today—my mother is a member of that flower club; I'm no gardener myself."

His tone implied a low opinion of male gardeners, which was none too bright if his idea was to get solid with Wolfe as well as Cramer.

He turned a palm up. "That's what brought me here. My mother came to see the orchids, and she invited Brown and his sister to come simply because she is good-hearted. But actually she doesn't know them, she knows nothing about them, because what they have told her is one thing and what they really are is something else. Then this happened, and in the past hour, after she recovered a little from the shock of being taken in there to identify the corpse, I have explained to her what the situation is."

He put his hands on the table and leaned on them, forward at Cramer. "I'm going to be quite frank, Inspector. Under the circumstances, I can't see that it would serve any useful purpose to let it be published that that woman came here with my mother. What good would it do? How would it further the cause of justice? I want to make it perfectly clear that we have no desire to evade our responsibility as citizens. But how would it help to get my mother's name in the headlines?"

He straightened, backed up a step, and looked affectionately at Mother.

"Names in headlines aren't what I'm after," Cramer told him, "but I don't run the newspapers. If they've already got it I can't stop them. I'd like to say I appreciate your frankness. So you only met Miss Brown a week ago. How many times had you seen her altogether?"

Three times, Gene said. Cramer had plenty of questions for both mother and son. It was in the middle of them that Wolfe passed me a slip of paper on which he had scribbled:

Tell Fritz to bring sandwiches and coffee for you and me. Also for those left in the front room. No one else. Of course Saul and Theodore.

I left the room, found Fritz in the kitchen, delivered the message, and returned.

Gene stayed cooperative to the end, and Mrs. Orwin tried, though it was an effort. They said they had been together all the time, which I happened to know wasn't so, having seen them separated at least twice during the afternoon—and Cramer did too, since I had told him. They said a lot of other things, among them that they hadn't left the plant rooms between their arrival and their departure with Wolfe; that they had stayed until most of the others were gone because Mrs. Orwin wanted to persuade Wolfe to sell her some plants; that Colonel Brown had wandered off by himself once or twice; that they had been only mildly concerned about Cynthia's absence because of assurances from Colonel Brown and me; and so on and so forth. Before they left, Gene made another try for a commitment to keep his mother's name out of it, and Cramer appreciated his frankness so much that he promised to do his best. I couldn't blame Cramer; people like them might be in a position to call almost anybody, even the commissioner or the mayor, by his first name.

Fritz had brought trays for Wolfe and me, and we were making headway with them. In the silence that followed the departure of the Orwins, Wolfe could plainly be heard chewing a mouthful of mixed salad.

Cramer sat frowning at us. He spoke not to Wolfe but to me. "Is that imported ham?"

I shook my head and swallowed before I answered. "No, Georgia. Pigs fed on peanuts and acorns. Cured to Mr. Wolfe's specifications. It smells good but it tastes even better. I'll copy the recipe for you—no, damn it, I can't, because the typewriter's in the office. Sorry." I put the sandwich down and picked up another. "I like to alternate—first a bit of ham, then sturgeon, then ham, then sturgeon . . ."

I could see him controlling himself. He turned his head. "Levy! Get that Colonel Brown in."

"Yes, sir. That man you wanted—Vedder—he's here."

"Then I'll take him first."

VI

Up in the plant rooms Malcolm Vedder had caught my eye by the way he picked up a flowerpot and held it. As he took a chair across the dining table from Cramer and me, I still thought he was worth another good look, but after his answer to Cramer's third question I relaxed and concentrated on my sandwiches. He was an actor and had had parts in three Broadway plays. Of course that explained it. No actor would pick up a flowerpot just normally, like you or me. He would have to dramatize it some way, and Vedder had happened to choose a way that looked to me like fingers closing around a throat.

Now he was dramatizing this by being wrought up and indignant about the cops dragging him into an investigation of a sensational murder. He kept running the long fingers of both his elegant hands through his

hair in a way that looked familiar, and I remembered I
had seen him the year before as the artist guy in *The
Primitives*.

"Typical!" he told Cramer, his eyes flashing and his
voice throaty with feeling. "Typical of police clumsi-
ness! Pulling *me* into this! The newspapermen out
front recognized me, of course, and the damned photographers! My God!"

"Yeah," Cramer said sympathetically. "It'll be
tough for an actor, having your picture in the paper.
We need help, us clumsy police, and you were among
those present. You're a member of this flower club?"

No, Vedder said, he wasn't. He had come with a
friend, a Mrs. Beauchamp, and when she had left to
keep an appointment he had remained to look at more
orchids. If only he had departed with her he would
have avoided this dreadful publicity. They had arrived
about three-thirty, and he had remained in the plant
rooms continuously until leaving with me at his heels.
He had seen no one that he had ever known or seen
before, except Mrs. Beauchamp. He knew nothing of
any Cynthia Brown or Colonel Percy Brown. Cramer
went through all the regulation questions and got all
the expected negatives, until he suddenly asked, "Did
you know Doris Hatten?"

Vedder frowned. "Who?"

"Doris Hatten. She was also—"

"Ah!" Vedder cried. "She was also strangled! I remember!"

"Right."

Vedder made fists of his hands, rested them on the
table, and leaned forward. His eyes had flashed again
and then gone dead. "You know," he said tensely,
"that's the worst of all, strangling—especially a
woman." His fists opened, the fingers spread apart,

and he gazed at them. "Imagine strangling a beautiful woman!"

"Did you know Doris Hatten?"

"Othello," Vedder said in a deep resonant tone. His eyes lifted to Cramer, and his voice lifted too. "No, I didn't know her; I only read about her." He shuddered all over and then, abruptly, he was out of his chair and on his feet. "Damn it all," he protested shrilly, "I only came here to look at orchids! God!"

He ran his fingers through his hair, turned, and made for the door. Levy looked at Cramer with his brows raised, and Cramer shook his head impatiently.

I muttered at Wolfe, "He hammed it, maybe?"

Wolfe wasn't interested.

The next one in was Bill McNab, garden editor of the *Gazette*. I knew him a little, but not well, most of my newspaper friends not being on garden desks. He looked unhappier than any of the others, even Mrs. Orwin, as he walked across to the table, to the end where Wolfe sat.

"I can't tell you how much I regret this, Mr. Wolfe," he said miserably.

"Don't try," Wolfe growled.

"I wish I could, I certainly do. What a really, really terrible thing! I wouldn't have dreamed such a thing could happen—the Manhattan Flower Club! Of course, she wasn't a member, but that only makes it worse in a way." McNab turned to Cramer. "I'm responsible for this."

"You are?"

"Yes. It was my idea. I persuaded Mr. Wolfe to arrange it. He let me word the invitations. And I was congratulating myself on the great success! The club has only a hundred and eighty-nine members, and there were over two hundred people here. Then this!

What can I do?" He turned. "I want you to know this, Mr. Wolfe. I got a message from my paper; they wanted me to do a story on it for the news columns, and I refused point-blank. Even if I get fired—I don't think I will."

"Sit down a minute," Cramer invited him.

McNab varied the monotony on one detail, at least. He admitted that he had left the plant rooms three times during the afternoon, once to accompany a departing guest down to the ground floor, and twice to go down alone to check on who had come and who hadn't. Aside from that, he was more of the same. He had never heard of Cynthia Brown. By now it was beginning to seem not only futile but silly to spend time on seven or eight of them merely because they happened to be the last to go and so were at hand. Also it was something new to me from a technical standpoint. I had never seen one stack up like that. Any precinct dick knows that every question you ask of everybody is aimed at one of the three targets: motive, means, and opportunity. In this case there were no questions to ask because those were already answered. Motive: the guy had followed her downstairs, knowing she had recognized him, had seen her enter Wolfe's office and thought she was doing exactly what she was doing, getting set to tell Wolfe, and had decided to prevent that the quickest and best way he knew. Means: any piece of cloth; even his handkerchief would do. Opportunity: he was there—all of them on Saul's list were.

So if you wanted to learn who strangled Cynthia Brown, first you had to find out who had strangled Doris Hatten, and the cops had already been working on that for five months.

As soon as Bill McNab had been sent on his way, Colonel Percy Brown was brought in.

Brown was not exactly at ease, but he had himself well in hand. You would never have picked him for a con man, and neither would I. His mouth and jaw were strong and attractive, and as he sat down he leveled his keen gray eyes at Cramer and kept them there. He wasn't interested in Wolfe or me. He said his name was Colonel Percy Brown, and Cramer asked him which army he was a colonel in.

"I think," Brown said in a cool even tone, "it will save time if I state my position. I will answer fully and freely all questions that relate to what I saw or heard or did since I arrived here this afternoon. To that extent I'll help you all I can. Answers to any other questions will have to wait until I consult my attorney."

Cramer nodded. "I expected that. The trouble is I'm pretty sure I don't give a damn what you saw or heard this afternoon. We'll come back to that. I want to put something to you. As you see, I'm not even wanting to know why you tried to break away before we got here."

"I merely wanted to phone—"

"Forget it." Cramer put the remains of his second cigar, not more than a scraggly inch, in the ashtray. "On information received, I think it's like this. The woman who called herself Cynthia Brown, murdered here today, was not your sister. You met her in Florida six or eight weeks ago. She went in with you on an operation of which Mrs. Orwin was the subject, and you introduced her to Mrs. Orwin as your sister. You two came to New York with Mrs. Orwin a week ago, with the operation well under way. As far as I'm concerned, that is only background. Otherwise I'm not interested in it. My work is homicide, and that's what I'm working on now."

Brown was listening politely.

"For me," Cramer went on, "the point is that for quite a period you have been closely connected with this Miss Brown, associating with her in a confidential operation. You must have had many intimate conversations with her. You were having her with you as your sister, and she wasn't, and she's been murdered. We could give you merry hell on that score alone."

Brown had no use for his tongue. His face said no comment.

"It'll never be too late to give you hell," Cramer assured him, "but I wanted to give you a chance first. For two months you've been on intimate terms with Cynthia Brown. She certainly must have mentioned an experience she had last October. A friend of hers named Doris Hatten was murdered—strangled. Cynthia Brown had information about the murderer which she kept to herself; if she had come out with it she'd be alive now. She must have mentioned that to you; you can't tell me she didn't. She must have told you all about it. Now you can tell me. If you do we can nail him for what he did here today, and it might even make things a little smoother for you. Well?"

Brown had pursed his lips. They straightened out again, and his hand came up for a finger to scratch his cheek.

"I'm sorry," he said.

"For what?"

"I'm sorry I can't help."

"Do you expect me to believe that during all those weeks she never mentioned the murder of her friend Doris Hatten?"

"I'm sorry I can't help."

Cramer got out another cigar and rolled it between his palms, which was wasted energy since he didn't intend to draw smoke through it. Having seen him do it before, I knew what it meant. He still thought he might get something from this customer and was taking time out to control himself.

"I'm sorry too," he said, trying not to make it a growl. "But she must have told you something of her previous career, didn't she?"

"I'm sorry." Brown's tone was firm and final.

"Okay. We'll move on to this afternoon. On that you said you'd answer fully and freely. Do you remember a moment when something about Cynthia Brown's appearance—some movement she made or the expression on her face—caused Mrs. Orwin to ask her what was the matter with her?"

A crease was showing on Brown's forehead. "I don't believe I do," he stated.

"I'm asking you to try. Try hard."

Silence. Brown pursed his lips and the crease in his forehead deepened. Finally he said, "I may not have been right there at the moment. In those aisles—in a crowd like that—we weren't rubbing elbows continuously."

"You do remember when she excused herself because she wasn't feeling well?"

"Yes, of course."

"Well, this moment I'm asking about came shortly before that. She exchanged looks with some man nearby, and it was her reaction to that that made Mrs. Orwin ask her what was the matter. What I'm interested in is that exchange of looks. If you saw it and can remember it, and can describe the man she exchanged looks with, I wouldn't give a damn if you stripped Mrs. Orwin clean and ten more like her."

"I didn't see it."

"You didn't."

"No."

"You didn't say you're sorry."

"I am, of course, if it would help—"

"To hell with you!" Cramer banged his fist on the table so hard the trays danced. "Levy! Take him out and tell Stebbins to send him down and lock him up. Material witness. Put more men on him. He's got a record somewhere. Find it!"

"I wish to phone my attorney," Brown said quietly but emphatically.

"There's a phone down where you're going," Levy told him. "If it's not out of order. This way, Colonel."

As the door closed behind them Cramer glared at me as if daring me to say that I was sorry too. Letting my face show how bored I was, I remarked casually, "If I could get in the office I'd show you a swell book on disguises; I forget the name of it. The world record is sixteen years—a guy in Italy fooled a brother and two cousins who had known him well. So maybe you ought to—"

Cramer turned from me rudely and said, "Gather up, Murphy. We're leaving." He shoved his chair back, stood up, and shook his ankles to get his pants legs down. Levy came back in, and Cramer addressed him. "We're leaving. Everybody out. To my office. Tell Stebbins one man out front will be enough—no, I'll tell him—"

"There's one more, sir."

"One more what?"

"In the front room. A man."

"Who?"

"His name is Nicholson Morley. He's a psychiatrist."

"Let him go. This is a goddam joke."

"Yes, sir."

Levy went. The shorthand dick had collected notebooks and other papers and was putting them into a battered briefcase. Cramer looked at Wolfe. Wolfe looked back at him.

"A while ago," Cramer rasped, "you said something had occurred to you."

"Did I?" Wolfe inquired coldly.

Their eyes went on clashing until Cramer broke the connection by turning to go. I restrained an impulse to knock their heads together. They were both being childish. If Wolfe really had something, anything at all, he knew damn well Cramer would gladly trade the seals on the office doors for it sight unseen. And Cramer knew damn well he could make the deal himself with nothing to lose. But they were both too sore and stubborn to show any horse sense.

Cramer had circled the end of the table on his way out when Levy re-entered to report, "That man Morley insists on seeing you. He says it's vital."

Cramer halted, glowering. "What is he, a screwball?"

"I don't know, sir. He may be."

"Oh, bring him in." Cramer came back around the table to his chair.

VII

This was my first really good look at the middle-aged male with the mop of black hair. His quick-darting eyes were fully as black as his hair, and the appearance of his chin and jowls made it evident that his beard would have been likewise if he gave it half a chance. He sat down and was telling Cramer who and what he was.

Cramer nodded impatiently. "I know. You have something to say, Dr. Morley?"

"I have. Something vital."

"Let's hear it."

Morley got better settled in his chair. "First, I assume that no arrest has been made. Is that correct?"

"Yes—if you mean an arrest with a charge of murder."

"Have you a definite object of suspicion, with or without evidence in support?"

"If you mean am I ready to name the murderer, no. Are you?"

"I think I may be."

Cramer's chin went up. "Well? I'm in charge here."

Dr. Morley smiled. "Not quite so fast. The suggestion I have to offer is sound only with certain assumptions." He placed the tip of his right forefinger on the tip of his left little finger. "One: that you have no idea who committed this murder, and apparently you haven't." He moved over a finger. "Two: that this was not a commonplace crime with a commonplace discoverable motive." To the middle finger. "Three: that nothing is known to discredit the hypothesis that this girl—I understand from Mrs. Orwin that her name was Cynthia Brown—that she was strangled by the man who strangled Doris Hatten on October seventh last year. May I make those assumptions?"

"You can try. Why do you want to?"

Morley shook his head. "Not that I want to. That if I am permitted to, I have a suggestion. I wish to make it clear that I have great respect for the competence of the police, within proper limits. If the man who murdered Doris Hatten had been vulnerable to police techniques and resources, he would almost certainly have been caught. But he wasn't. You failed utterly. Why?"

"You're telling me."

"Because he was out of bounds for you. Because your exploration of motive is restricted by your preconceptions." Morley's black eyes gleamed. "You're a layman, so I won't use technical terms. The most powerful motives on earth are motives of the personality, which cannot be exposed by any purely objective investigation. If the personality is twisted, distorted, as it is with a psychotic, then the motives are twisted too. As a psychiatrist I was deeply interested in the published reports of the murder of Doris Hatten—especially the detail that she was strangled with her own scarf. When your efforts to find the culprit—thorough, no doubt, and even brilliant—ended in complete failure, I would have been glad to come forward with a suggestion, but I was as helpless as you."

"Get down to it," Cramer muttered.

"Yes." Morley put his elbows on the table and paired all his fingertips. "Now today. On the basis of the assumptions I began with, it is a tenable theory, worthy to be tested, that this was the same man. If so he has made a mistake. Apparently no one got in here today without having his name checked; the man at the door was most efficient. So it is no longer a question of finding him among thousands or millions; it's a mere hundred or so, and I am willing to contribute my services. I don't think there are more than three or four men in New York qualified for such a job, and I am one of them. You can verify that."

The black eyes flashed. "I admit that for a psychiatrist this is a rare opportunity. Nothing could be more dramatic than a psychosis exploding into murder. I don't pretend that my suggestion is entirely unselfish. All you have to do is to have them brought to my office —one at a time, of course. With some of them ten minutes will be enough, but with others it may take hours. When I have—"

"Wait a minute," Cramer put in. "Are you suggesting that we deliver everyone that was here today to your office for you to work on?"

"No, not everyone, only the men. When I have finished I may have nothing that can be used as evidence, but there's an excellent chance that I can tell you who the strangler is, and when you once know that—"

"Excuse me," Cramer said. He was on his feet. "Sorry to cut you off, Doctor, but I must get downtown." He was on his way. "I'm afraid your suggestion wouldn't work. I'll let you know—"

He went, and Levy and Murphy with him.

Dr. Morley pivoted his head to watch them go, kept it that way a moment, and then came back to us. He looked disappointed but not beaten. The black eyes, after resting on me briefly, darted to Wolfe.

"You," he said, "are intelligent and literate. I should have had you more in mind. May I count on you to explain to that policeman why my suggestion is the only hope for him?"

"No," Wolfe said curtly.

"He's had a hard day," I told Morley. "So have I. Would you mind closing the door after you?"

He looked as if he had a notion to start on me as a last resort, so I got up and circled around to the door, which had been left open, and remarked to him, "This way, please."

He arose and walked out without a word. I shut the door, had a good stretch and yawn, crossed to open a window and stick my head out for a breath of air, closed the window, and looked at my wrist watch.

"Twenty minutes to ten," I announced.

Wolfe muttered, "Go look at the office door."

"I just did, as I let Morley out. It's sealed. Malefic spite."

"See if they're gone and bolt the door. Send Saul home and tell him to come at nine in the morning. Tell Fritz I want beer."

I obeyed. The hall and front room were uninhabited. Saul, whom I found in the kitchen with Fritz, said he had made a complete tour upstairs and everything was in order. I stayed for a little chat with him while Fritz took a tray to the dining room. When I left him and went back Wolfe, removing the cap from a bottle of beer with the opener Fritz had brought on the tray, was making a face, which I understood. The opener he always used, a gold item that a satisfied client had given him years ago, was in the drawer of his desk in the office. I sat and watched him pour beer.

"This isn't a bad room to sit in," I said brightly.

"Pfui! I want to ask you something."

"Shoot."

"I want your opinion of this. Assume that we accept without reservation the story Miss Brown told you. By the way, do you?"

"In view of what happened, yes."

"Then assume it. Assume also that the man she had recognized, knowing she had recognized him, followed her downstairs and saw her enter the office; that he surmised that she intended to consult me; that he postponed joining her in the office either because he knew you were in there with her or for some other reason; that he saw you come out and go upstairs; that he took an opportunity to enter the office unobserved, got her off guard, killed her, got out unobserved, and returned upstairs. All of those assumptions seem to be required, unless we discard all that and dig elsewhere."

"I'll take it that way."

"Very well. Then we have significant indications of his character. Consider it. He has killed her and is back upstairs, knowing that she was in the office talking with you for some time. He would like to know what she said to you. Specifically, he would like to know whether she told you about him, and if so how much. Had she or had she not named or described him in his current guise? With that question unanswered, would a man of his character as indicated leave the house? Or would he prefer the challenge and risk of remaining until the body had been discovered, to see what you would do? And I too, of course, after you had talked with me, and the police?"

"Yeah." I chewed my lip. There was a long silence. "So that's how your mind's working. I could offer a guess."

"I prefer a calculation to a guess. For that a basis is needed, and we have it. We know the situation as we have assumed it, and we know something of his character."

"Okay," I conceded, "a calculation. I'll be damned. The answer I get, he would stick around until the body was found, and if he did, then he is one of the bunch Cramer has been talking with. So that's what occurred to you, huh?"

"No. By no means. That's a different matter. This is merely a tentative calculation for a starting point. If it is sound, I know who the murderer is."

I gave him a look. Sometimes I can tell how much he is putting on and sometimes I can't. I decided to buy it. With the office sealed up by the crabbed and envious mind of Inspector Cramer, he was certainly in no condition to entertain himself by trying to string me.

"That's interesting," I said admiringly. "If you

want me to get him on the phone I'll have to use the one in the kitchen."

"I want to test the calculation."

"So do I."

"But there's a difficulty. The test I have in mind, the only one I can contrive to my satisfaction—only you can make it. And in doing so you would have to expose yourself to great personal risk."

"For God's sake." I gawked at him. "This is a brand-new one. The errands you've sent me on! Since when have you flinched or faltered in the face of danger to me?"

"This danger is extreme."

"So is the fix you're in. The office is sealed, and in it are the book you're reading and the television set. Let's hear the test. Describe it. All I ask is ninety-nine chances in a hundred."

"Very well." He turned a hand over. "The decision will be yours. The typewriter in the office is inaccessible. Is that old one in your room in working order?"

"Fair."

"Bring it down here, and some sheets of blank paper—any kind. I'll need a blank envelope."

"I have some."

"Bring one. Also the telephone book, Manhattan, from my room."

I went to the hall and up two flights of stairs. Having collected the first three items in my room, I descended a flight, found that the door of Wolfe's room was still locked, and had to put the typewriter on the floor to get out my keys. With a full cargo I returned to the dining room, unloaded, and was placing the typewriter in position on the table when Wolfe spoke.

"No, bring it here. I'll use it myself."

I lifted my brows at him. "A page will take you an hour."

"It won't be a page. Put a sheet of paper in it."

I did so, got the paper squared, lifted the machine, and put it in front of him. He sat and frowned at it for a long minute and then started pecking. I turned my back on him to make it easier to withhold remarks about his two-finger technique, and passed the time by trying to figure his rate. That was hopeless, because at one moment he would be going at about twelve words a minute and then would come a sudden burst of speed, stepping it up to twenty or more. All at once there was the sound of the ratchet turning as he pulled the paper out, and I supposed he had ruined it and was going to start over, but when I turned to look his hand was extended to me with the sheet in it.

"I think that will do," he said.

I took it and read what he had typed:

She told me enough this afternoon so that I know who to send this to, and more. I have kept it to myself because I haven't decided what is the right thing to do. I would like to have a talk with you first, and if you will phone me tomorrow, Tuesday, between nine o'clock and noon, we can make an appointment; please don't put it off or I will have to decide myself.

I read it over three times. I looked at Wolfe. He had put an envelope in the typewriter and was consulting the phone book.

"It's all right," I said, "except that I don't care for the semicolon after 'appointment.' I would have put a period and started a new sentence."

He began pecking, addressing the envelope. I

waited until he had finished and rolled the envelope out.

"Just like this?" I asked. "No name or initials signed?"

"No."

"I admit it's nifty," I admitted. "Hell, we could forget the calculation and send this to every guy on that list and wait to see who phoned. He has just about got to phone—and also make a date."

"I prefer to send it only to one person—the one indicated by your report of that conversation. That will test the calculation."

"And save postage." I glanced at the paper. "The extreme danger, I suppose, is that I'll get strangled. Or of course in an emergency like this he might try something else. He might even arrange for help. If you want me to mail this I'll need that envelope."

"I don't want to minimize the risk of this, Archie."

"Neither do I. I'll have to borrow a gun from Saul; ours are in the office. May I have that envelope? I'll have to go to Times Square to mail it."

"Yes. Before you do so, copy that note; we should have a copy. Keep Saul here in the morning. If and when the phone call comes you will have to use your wits to arrange the appointment as advantageously as possible. Discussion of plans will have to wait upon that."

"Right. The envelope, please?"

He handed it to me.

VIII

As far as Wolfe was concerned, the office being sealed made no difference in the morning up to eleven o'clock,

since his schedule had him in the plant rooms from nine
to eleven. With me it did. From breakfast on was the
best time for my office chores, including the morning
mail.

That Tuesday morning, however, it didn't matter
much, since I was kept busy from eight o'clock on by
the phone and the doorbell. After nine Saul was there
to help, but not with the phone because the orders
were that I was to answer all calls. They were mostly
from newspapers, but there were a couple from Homicide—once Rowcliff and once Purley Stebbins—and a
few scattered ones, including one with comic relief
from the president of the Manhattan Flower Club. I
took them on the extension in the kitchen. Every time
I lifted the thing and told the transmitter, "Nero
Wolfe's office, Archie Goodwin speaking," my pulse
went up a notch and then had to level off again. I had
one argument, with a bozo in the District Attorney's
office who had the strange idea that he could order me
to report for an interview at eleven-thirty sharp,
which ended by my agreeing to call later to fix an hour.

A little before eleven I was in the kitchen with
Saul, who at Wolfe's direction had been briefed to date,
trying to come to terms on a bet. I was offering him
even money that the call would come by noon and he
was holding out for five to three, having originally
asked for two to one. I was suggesting sarcastically
that we change sides when the phone rang and I got it
and said distinctly, "Nero Wolfe's office, Archie Goodwin speaking."

"Mr. Goodwin?"

"Right."

"You sent me a note."

My hand wanted to grip the phone the way Vedder
had gripped the flowerpot, but I wouldn't let it.

"Did I? What about?"

"You suggested that we make an appointment. Are you in a position to discuss it?"

"Sure. I'm alone and no extensions are on. But I don't recognize your voice. Who is this?"

That was just putting a nickel's worth of breath on a long shot. Saul, at a signal from me, had raced up to the extension in Wolfe's room, and this bird might possibly be completely loony. But no.

"I have two voices. This is the other one. Have you made a decision yet?"

"No. I was waiting to hear from you."

"That's wise, I think. I'm willing to discuss the matter. Are you free for this evening?"

"I can wiggle free."

"With a car to drive?"

"Yeah, I have a car."

"Drive to a lunchroom at the northeast corner of Fifty-first Street and Eleventh Avenue. Get there at eight o'clock. Park your car on Fifty-first Street, but not at the corner. Got that?"

"Yes."

"You will be alone, of course. Go in the lunchroom and order something to eat. I won't be there, but you will get a message. You'll be there at eight o'clock?"

"Yes. I still don't recognize your voice. I don't think you're the person I sent the note to."

"I am. It's good, isn't it?"

The connection went.

I hung up, told Fritz he could answer calls now, and hot-footed it to the stairs and up a flight. Saul was there on the landing.

"Whose voice was that?" I demanded.

"Search me. You heard all I did." His eyes had a gleam in them, and I suppose mine did too.

"Whoever it was," I said, "I've got a date. Let's go up and tell the genius. I've got to admit he saved a lot of postage."

We mounted the other two flights and found Wolfe in the cool room, inspecting a bench of dendrobiums for damage from the invasion of the day before. When I told him about the call he merely nodded, not even taking the trouble to smirk, as if picking a murderer first crack out of ten dozen men was the sort of thing he did between yawns.

"That call," he said, "validates our assumptions and verifies our calculation, but that's all. If it had done more than that it wouldn't have been made. Has anyone come to take those seals off?"

I told him no. "I asked Stebbins about it and he said he'd ask Cramer."

"Don't ask again," he snapped. "We'll go down to my room."

If the strangler had been in Wolfe's house the rest of that day he would have felt honored—or anyway he should. Even during Wolfe's afternoon hours in the plant rooms, from four to six, his mind was on my appointment, as was proved by the crop of new slants and ideas that poured out of him when he came down to the kitchen. Except for a trip to Leonard Street to answer an hour's worth of questions by an assistant district attorney, my day was devoted to it too. My most useful errand, though at the time it struck me as a waste of time and money, was one made to Doc Vollmer for a prescription and then to a drugstore under instructions from Wolfe.

When I got back from the D.A.'s office Saul and I got in the sedan and went for a reconnaissance. We didn't stop at Fifty-first Street and Eleventh Avenue, but drove past it four times. The main idea was to find a place for Saul. He and Wolfe both insisted that he had to be there with his eyes and ears open, and I insisted that he had to be covered enough not to scare off my date, who could spot his big nose a mile off. We finally settled for a filling station across the street from the lunchroom. Saul was to have a taxi drive in there at eight o'clock, and stay in the passenger's seat while the driver tried to get his carburetor adjusted. There were so many contingencies to be agreed on that if it had been anyone but Saul I wouldn't have expected him to remember more than half. For instance, in case I left the lunchroom and got in my car and drove off Saul was not to follow unless I cranked my window down.

Trying to provide for contingencies was okay in a way, but at seven o'clock, as the three of us sat in the dining room, finishing the roast duck, I had the feeling that we might as well have spent the day playing pool. Actually it was strictly up to me, since I had to let the other guy make the rules until and unless it got to where I felt I could take over and win. And with the other guy making the rules no one gets very far, not even Nero Wolfe, arranging for contingencies ahead of time; you meet them as they come, and if you meet one wrong it's too bad.

Saul left before I did, to find a taxi driver that he liked the looks of. When I went to the hall for my hat and raincoat, Wolfe came along, and I was really touched, since he wasn't through yet with his after-dinner coffee.

"I still don't like the idea," he insisted, "of your having that thing in your pocket. I think you should slip it inside your sock."

"I don't." I was putting the raincoat on. "If I get frisked, a sock is as easy to feel as a pocket."

"You're sure that gun is loaded?"

"For God's sake. I never saw you so anxious. Next you'll be telling me to put on my rubbers."

He even opened the door for me.

It wasn't actually raining, merely trying to make up its mind whether to or not, but after a couple of blocks I reached to switch on the windshield wiper. As I turned uptown on Tenth Avenue the dash clock said 7:47; as I turned left on Fifty-first Street it had only got to 7:51. At that time of day in that district there was plenty of space, and I rolled to the curb and stopped about twenty yards short of the corner, stopped the engine and turned off the lights, and cranked my window down for a good view of the filling station across the street. There was no taxi there. I glanced at my wrist watch and relaxed. At 7:59 a taxi pulled in and stopped by the pumps, and the driver got out and lifted the hood and started peering. I put my window up, locked three doors, pulled the key out, got myself out, locked the door, walked to the lunchroom, and entered.

There was one hash slinger behind the counter and five customers scattered along on the stools. I picked a stool that left me elbow room, sat, and ordered ice cream and coffee. That made me slightly conspicuous in those surroundings, but I refused to insult Fritz's roast duck, which I could still taste. The counterman served me and I took my time. At 8:12 the ice cream was gone and my cup empty, and I ordered a refill. I had about got to the end of that too when a male entered, looked along the line, came straight to me, and asked me what my name was. I told him, and he handed me a folded piece of paper and turned to go.

He was barely old enough for high school, and I made no effort to hold him, thinking that the bird I had a date with was not likely to be an absolute sap. Unfolding the paper, I saw neatly printed in pencil:

Go to your car and get a note under the windshield wiper. Sit in the car to read it.

I paid what I owed, walked to my car and got the note as I was told, unlocked the car and got in, turned on the light, and read in the same print:

Make no signal of any kind. Follow instructions precisely. Turn right on 11th Ave. and go slowly to 56th St. Turn right on 56th and go to 9th Ave. Turn right on 9th Ave. Right again on 45th. Left on 11th Ave. Left on 38th. Right on 7th Ave. Right on 27th St. Park on 27th between 9th and 10th Aves. Go to No. 814 and tap five times on the door. Give the man who opens the door this note and the other one. He will tell you where to go.

I didn't like it much, but I had to admit it was a handy arrangement for seeing to it that I went to the conference unattached or there wouldn't be any conference. It had now decided to rain. Starting the engine, I could see dimly through the misty window that Saul's taxi driver was still monkeying with his carburetor, but of course I had to resist the impulse to crank the window down to wave so long. Keeping the instructions in my left hand, I rolled to the corner, waited for the light to change, and turned right on Eleventh Avenue. Since I had not been forbidden to keep my eyes open I did so, and as I stopped at Fifty-second for the red light I saw a black or dark blue sedan pull away from the curb behind me and creep in my direction. I took it for granted that that was my chaperon, but even so I followed directions and kept to a crawl until I reached Fifty-sixth and turned right.

In spite of all the twistings and turnings and the lights we had to stop at, I didn't get the license number of the black sedan for certain until the halt at Thirty-eighth Street and Seventh Avenue. Not that that raised my pulse any, license plates not being welded on, but what the hell, I was a detective, wasn't I? It was at that same corner, seeing a flatfoot on the sidewalk, that I had half a notion to jump out, summon him, and tackle the driver of the sedan. If it was the strangler, I had the two printed notes in my possession, and I could at least have made it stick enough for an escorted trip to the Fourteenth Precinct Station for a chat. I voted it down, and was soon glad of it.

The guy in the sedan was not the strangler, as I soon learned. On Twenty-seventh Street there was space smack in front of Number 814 and I saw no reason why I shouldn't use it. The sedan went to the curb right behind me. After locking my car I stood on the sidewalk a moment, but my chaperon just sat tight, so I kept to the instructions, mounted the steps to the stoop of the run-down old brownstone, entered the vestibule, and knocked five times on the door. Through the glass panel the dimly lit hall looked empty. As I peered in, thinking I would either have to knock a lot louder or ignore instructions and ring the bell, I heard footsteps behind and turned. It was my chaperon.

"Well, we got here," I said cheerfully.

"You damn near lost me at one light," he said accusingly. "Give me them notes."

I handed them to him—all the evidence I had. As he unfolded them for a look I took him in. He was around my age and height, skinny but with muscles, with outstanding ears and a purple mole on his right jaw. If it was him I had a date with I sure had been diddled. "They look like it," he said, and stuffed the notes in a pocket. From another pocket he produced a key, unlocked the door, and pushed it open. "Follow me."

I did so, to the stairs and up. As we ascended two flights, with him in front, it would have been a cinch for me to reach and take a gun off his hip if there had been one there, but there wasn't. He may have preferred a shoulder holster like me. The stair steps were bare worn wood, the walls had needed plaster since at least Pearl Harbor, and the smell was a mixture I wouldn't want to analyze. On the second landing he went down the hall to a door at the rear, opened it, and signaled me through with a jerk of his head.

There was another man there, but still it wasn't my date—anyway I hoped not. It would be an overstatement to say the room was furnished, but I admit there was a table, a bed, and three chairs, one of them upholstered. The man, who was lying on the bed, pushed himself up as we entered, and as he swung around to sit, his feet barely reached the floor. He had shoulders and a torso like a heavyweight wrestler, and legs like an underweight jockey. His puffed eyes blinked in the light from the unshaded bulb as if he had been asleep.

"That him?" he demanded and yawned.

Skinny said it was. The wrestler-jockey, W-J for short, got up and went to the table, picked up a ball of thick cord, approached me and spoke. "Take off your hat and coat and sit there." He pointed to one of the straight chairs.

"Hold it," Skinny commanded him. "I haven't explained yet." He faced me. "The idea is simple. This man that's coming to see you don't want any trouble.

He just wants to talk. So we tie you in that chair and leave you, and he comes and you have a talk, and after he leaves we come back and cut you loose and out you go. Is that plain enough?"

I grinned at him. "It sure is, brother. It's too damn plain. What if I won't sit down? What if I wiggle when you start to tie me?"

"Then he don't come and you don't have a talk."

"What if I walk out now?"

"Go ahead. We get paid anyhow. If you want to see this guy, there's only one way: we tie you in the chair."

"We get more if we tie him," W-J objected. "Let me persuade him."

"Lay off," Skinny commanded him.

"I don't want any trouble either," I stated. "How about this? I sit in the chair and you fix the cord to look right but so I'm free to move in case of fire. There's a hundred bucks in the wallet in my breast pocket. Before you leave you help yourselves."

"A lousy C?" W-J sneered. "For Chrissake shut up and sit down."

"He has his choice," Skinny said reprovingly.

I did indeed. It was a swell illustration of how much good it does to try to consider contingencies in advance. In all our discussions that day none of us had put the question, what to do if a pair of smooks offered me my pick of being tied in a chair or going home to bed. As far as I could see, standing there looking them over, that was all there was to it, and it was too early to go home to bed.

Thinking it would help to know whether they really were smooks or merely a couple of rummies on the payroll of some fly-specked agency, I decided to try something. Not letting my eyes know what my hand was about to do, I suddenly reached inside my coat to

the holster, and then they had something more interesting than my face to look at: Saul's clean shiny automatic.

The wrestler-jockey put his hands up high and
froze. Skinny looked irritated.

"For why?" he demanded.

"I thought we might all go for a walk down to my
car. Then to the Fourteenth Precinct, which is the closest."

"What do we do then?"

There he had me.

"You either want to see this guy or you don't,"
Skinny explained patiently. "Seeing how you got that
gun out, I guess he must know you. I don't blame him
wanting your hands arranged for." He turned his
palms up. "Make up your mind."

I put the gun back in the holster, took off my hat
and raincoat and hung them on a hook on the wall,
moved one of the straight chairs so the light wouldn't
glare in my eyes, and sat.

"Okay," I told them, "but by God don't overdo it. I
know my way around and I can find you if I care
enough, don't think I can't."

They unrolled the cord, cutting pieces off, and went
to work. W-J tied my left wrist to the rear left leg of
the chair while Skinny did the right. They were both
thorough, but to my surprise Skinny was rougher. I
insisted it was too tight, and he gave a stingy thirty-
second of an inch. They wanted to do my ankles the
same way, to the bottoms of the front legs of the chair,
but I claimed I would get cramps sitting like that, and
I was already fastened to the chair, and it would be
just as good to tie my ankles together. They discussed
it, and I had my way. Skinny made a final inspection of
the knots and then went over me. He took the gun

from my shoulder holster and tossed it on the bed, made sure I didn't have another one, and left the room.

W-J picked up the gun and scowled at it. "These goddam things," he muttered. "They make more trouble." He went to the table and put the gun down on it, tenderly, as if it were something that might break. Then he crossed to the bed and stretched out on it.

"How long do we have to wait?" I asked.

"Not long. I wasn't to bed last night." He closed his eyes.

He got no nap. His barrel chest couldn't have gone up and down more than a dozen times before the door opened and Skinny came in. With him was a man in a gray pin-stripe suit and a dark gray Homburg, with a gray topcoat over his arm. He had gloves on. W-J got off the bed and onto his toothpick legs. Skinny stood by the open door. The man put his hat and coat on the bed, came and took a look at my fastenings, and told Skinny, "All right, I'll come for you." The two rummies departed, shutting the door. The man stood facing me, looking down at me, and I looked back.

He smiled. "Would you have known me?"

"Not from Adam," I said, both to humor him and because it was true.

IX

I wouldn't want to exaggerate how brave I am. It wasn't that I was too damn fearless to be impressed by the fact that I was thoroughly tied up and the strangler was standing there smiling at me: I was simply astounded. It was an amazing disguise. The two main changes were the eyebrows and eyelashes; these eyes had bushy brows and long thick lashes, whereas yesterday's guest hadn't had much of either one. The real change was from the inside. I had seen no smile on the face of yesterday's guest, but if I had it wouldn't have been like this one. The hair made a difference too, of course, parted on the side and slicked down.

He pulled the other straight chair around and sat. I admired the way he moved. That in itself could have been a dead giveaway, but the movements fitted the getup to a T. Finding the light straight in his eyes, he shifted the chair a little.

"So she told you about me?" he said, making it a question.

It was the voice he had used on the phone. It was actually different, pitched lower for one thing, but with it, as with the face and movements, the big change was from the inside. The voice was stretched tight, and the palms of his gloved hands were pressed against his kneecaps with the fingers straight out.

I said, "Yes," and added conversationally, "When you saw her go in the office why didn't you follow her in? Why did you wait?"

"That isn't—" he said, and stopped.

I waited politely.

He spoke. "I had seen you leave, upstairs, and I suspected you were in there."

"Why didn't she scream or fight?"

"I talked to her. I talked a little first." His head gave a quick jerk, as if a fly were bothering him and his hands were too occupied to attend to it. "What did she tell you?"

"About that day at Doris Hatten's apartment—you coming in and her going out. And of course her recognizing you there yesterday."

"She is dead. There is no evidence. You can't prove anything."

I grinned. "Then you're wasting a lot of time and energy and the best disguise I ever saw. Why didn't you just toss my note in the wastebasket? Let me answer. You didn't dare. In getting evidence, knowing exactly what and who to look for makes all the difference. And you knew I knew."

"And you haven't told the police?"

"No."

"Nor Nero Wolfe?"

"No."

"Why not?"

I shrugged—not much of a shrug, on account of my status quo. "I may not put it very well," I said, "because this is the first time I have ever talked with my hands and feet tied and I find it cramps my style. But it strikes me as the kind of coincidence that doesn't happen very often. I'm fed up with the detective business and I'd like to quit. I have something that's worth a good deal to you—say fifty thousand dollars. It can be arranged so that you get what you pay for. I'll go the limit on that, but it has to be closed damn quick. If you don't buy I'm going to have a tough time explaining why I didn't remember sooner what she told me. Twenty-four hours from now is the absolute limit."

"It couldn't be arranged so I would get what I paid for."

"Sure it could. If you don't want me on your neck the rest of your life, believe me, I don't want you on mine either."

"I suppose you don't." He smiled, or at least he apparently thought he was smiling. "I suppose I'll have to pay."

There was a sudden noise in his throat as if he had started to choke. He stood up. "You're working your hand loose," he said huskily and moved toward me.

It might have been guessed from his voice, thick and husky from the blood rushing to his head, but it was plain as day in his eyes, suddenly fixed and glassy like a blind man's eyes. Evidently he had come there fully intending to kill me and had now worked himself up to it. I felt a crazy impulse to laugh. Kill me with what?

"Hold it!" I snapped at him.

He halted, muttered, "You're getting your hand loose," and moved again, passing me to get behind.

With what purchase I could get on the floor with my bound feet, I jerked my body and the chair violently aside and around and had him in front of me again.

"No good," I told him. "They only went down one flight. I heard 'em. It's no good anyway. I've got another note for you—from Nero Wolfe—here in my breast pocket. Help yourself, but stay in front of me."

His eyes stayed glassy on me.

"Don't you want to know what it says?" I demanded. "Get it!"

He was only two steps from me, but it took him four small slow ones. His gloved hand went inside my coat to the breast pocket, and came out with a folded slip of yellow paper—a sheet from one of Wolfe's memo pads. From the way his eyes looked, I doubted if he would be able to read, but apparently he was. I watched his face as he took it in, in Wolfe's straight precise handwriting:

If Mr. Goodwin is not home by midnight the information given him by Cynthia Brown will be communicated to the police and I shall see that they act immediately.

Nero Wolfe

He looked at me, and slowly his eyes changed. No longer glassy, they began to let light in. Before he had just been going to kill me. Now he hated me.

I got voluble. "So it's no good, see? He did it this way because if you had known I had told him you would have sat tight. He figured that you would think you could handle me, and I admit you tried your best. He wants fifty thousand dollars by tomorrow at six o'clock, no later. You say it can't be arranged so you'll get what you pay for, but we say it can and it's up to you. You say we have no evidence, but we can get it— don't you think we can't. As for me, I wouldn't advise you even to pull my hair. It would make him sore at you, and he's not sore now, he just wants fifty thousand bucks."

He had started to tremble and knew it, and was trying to stop.

"Maybe," I conceded, "you can't get that much that quick. In that case he'll take your IOU. You can write it on the back of that note he sent you. My pen's here in my vest pocket. He'll be reasonable about it."

"I'm not such a fool," he said harshly. He had stopped trembling.

"Who said you were?" I was sharp and urgent and thought I had loosened him. "Use your head, that's all. We've either got you cornered or we haven't. If we haven't, what are you doing here? If we have, a little thing like your name signed to an IOU won't make it any worse. He won't press you too hard. Here, get my pen, right here."

I still think I had loosened him. It was in his eyes and the way he stood, sagging a little. If my hands had been free, so I could have got the pen myself and un-capped it and put it between his fingers, I would have had him. I had him to the point of writing and signing, but not to the point of taking my pen out of my pocket. But of course if my hands had been free I wouldn't have been bothering about an IOU and a pen.

So he slipped from under. He shook his head, and his shoulders stiffened. The hate that filled his eyes was in his voice too. "You said twenty-four hours. That gives me tomorrow. I'll have to decide. Tell Nero Wolfe I'll decide."

He crossed to the door and pulled it open. He went out, closing the door, and I heard his steps descending the stairs; but he hadn't taken his hat and coat, and I nearly cracked my temples trying to use my brain. I hadn't got far when there were steps on the stairs again, coming up, and in they came, all three of them. W-J was blinking again; apparently there was a bed where they had been waiting. My host ignored him and spoke to Skinny.

"What time does your watch say?"

Skinny glanced at his wrist. "Nine-thirty-two."

"At half-past ten, not before that, untie his left hand. If he has a knife where he can get at it with his left hand, take it and—no, keep it. Leave him like that and go. It will take him five minutes or more to get his other hand and his feet free. Have you any objection to that?"

"Hell no. He's got nothing on us."

"Will you do it that way?"

"Right. Ten-thirty on the nose."

The strangler took a roll of bills from his pocket, having a little difficulty on account of his gloves, peeled off two twenties, went to the table with them, and gave them a good rub on both sides with his handkerchief.

He held the bills out to Skinny. "I've paid the

agreed amount, as you know. This extra is so you won't get impatient and leave before half-past ten."

"Don't take it!" I called sharply.

Skinny, the bills in his hand, turned. "What's the matter, they got germs?"

"No, but they're peanuts, you sap! He's worth ten grand to you! As is! Ten grand!"

"Nonsense," the strangler said scornfully and started for the bed to get his hat and coat.

"Gimme my twenty," W-J demanded.

Skinny stood with his head cocked, regarding me. He looked faintly interested but skeptical, and I saw it would take more than words. As the strangler picked up his hat and coat and turned, I jerked my body violently to the left and over I went, chair and all. I have no idea how I got across the floor to the door. I couldn't simply roll on account of the chair, I couldn't crawl without hands, and I didn't even try to jump. But I made it, and not slow, and was there, down on my right side, the chair against the door and me against the chair, before any of them snapped out of it enough to reach me.

"You think," I yapped at Skinny, "it's just a job? Let him go and you'll find out! Do you want his name? Mrs. Carlisle—Mrs. Homer N. Carlisle. Do you want her address?"

The strangler, on his way to me, stopped and froze. He—or I should say she—stood stiff as a bar of steel, the long-lashed eyes aimed at me.

"Missus?" Skinny demanded incredulously. "Did you say Missus?"

"Yes. She's a woman. I'm tied up, but you've got her. I'm helpless, so you can have her. You might give me a cut of the ten grand." The strangler made a movement. "Watch her!"

W-J, who had started for me and stopped, turned to face her. I had banged my head and it hurt. Skinny stepped to her, jerked both sides of her double-breasted coat open, released them, and backed up a step. "It could be a woman," he said judiciously.

"Hell, we can find that out easy enough." W-J moved. "Dumb as I am, I can tell *that*."

"Go ahead," I urged. "That will check her and me both. Go ahead!"

She made a noise in her throat. W-J got to her and put out a hand. She shrank away and screamed, "Don't touch me!"

"I'll be goddamned," W-J said wonderingly.

"What's this gag," Skinny demanded, "about ten grand?"

"It's a long story," I told him, "but it's there if you want it. If you'll cut me in for a third it's a cinch. If she gets out of here and gets safe home we can't touch her. All we have to do is connect her as she is—here now, disguised—with Mrs. Homer N. Carlisle, which is what she'll be when she gets home. If we do that we've got her shirt. As she is here now, she's red hot. As she is at home, you couldn't even get in."

I had to play it that way. I just didn't dare say call a cop, because if he felt about cops the way some rummies do he might have dragged me away from the door and let her go.

"So what?" Skinny asked. "I didn't bring my camera."

"I've got something better. Get me loose and I'll show you."

Skinny didn't like that. He eyed me a moment and turned for a look at the others. Mrs. Carlisle was backed against the bed, and W-J stood studying her

with his fists on his hips. Skinny returned to me. "I'll
do it. Maybe. What is it?"

"Damn it," I snapped, "at least put me right side
up. These cords are eating my wrists."

He came and got the back of the chair with one
hand and my arm with the other, and I clamped my
feet to the floor to give us leverage. He was stronger
than he looked. Upright on the chair again, I was still
blocking the door.

"Get a bottle," I told him, "out of my right-hand
coat pocket—no, here, the coat I've got on. I hope to
God it didn't break."

He fished it out. It was intact. He held it to the
light to read the label.

"What is it?"

"Silver nitrate. It makes a black indelible mark on
most things, including skin. Pull up her pants leg and
mark her with it."

"Then what?"

"Let her go. We'll have her. With the three of us
able to explain how and when she got marked, she's
sunk."

"How come you've got this stuff?"

"I was hoping for a chance to mark her myself."

"How much will it hurt her?"

"None at all. Put some on me—anywhere you like,
as long as it don't show."

"You'd better give me the story—why she'll be
sunk. I don't care how long it is."

"Not till she's marked." I was firm. "I will as soon
as you mark her."

He studied the label again. I watched his face, hoping he wouldn't ask if the mark would be permanent
because I didn't know what answer would suit him,
and I had to sell him.

"A woman," he muttered. "By God, a woman!"

"Yeah," I said sympathetically. "She sure made a monkey of you."

He swiveled his head and called, "Hey!"

W-J turned. Skinny commanded him, "Pin her up! Don't hurt her."

W-J reached for her. But, as he did so, all of a sudden she was neither man nor woman, but a cyclone. Her first leap, away from his reaching hand, was side-wise, and by the time he had realized he didn't have her she had got to the table and grabbed the gun. He made for her and she pulled the trigger and down he went, tumbling right at her feet. By that time Skinny was almost to her and she whirled and blazed away again. He kept going, and from the force of the blow on my left shoulder I might have calculated, if I had been in a mood for calculating, that the bullet had not gone through Skinny before it hit me. She pulled the trigger a third time, but by then Skinny had her wrist and was breaking her arm.

"She got me!" W-J was yelling indignantly. "She got me in the leg!"

Skinny had her down on her knees.

"Come and cut me loose," I called to him, "and give me that gun, and go find a phone."

Except for my wrists and ankles and shoulder and head, I felt fine all over.

X

"I hope you're satisfied," Inspector Cramer said sourly. "You and Goodwin have got your pictures in the paper again. You got no fee, but a lot of free public-ity. I got my nose wiped."

Wolfe grunted comfortably.

It was seven o'clock the next evening, and the three of us were in the office, me at the desk with my arm in a sling, Cramer in the red leather chair, and Wolfe on his throne back of his desk, with a glass of beer in his hand and a second unopened bottle on the tray in front of him. The seals had been removed by Sergeant Stebbins a little before noon, in between other chores. The whole squad had been busy with chores: visiting W-J at the hospital, conversing with Mr. and Mrs. Carlisle at the D.A.'s office, starting to round up circumstantial evidence to show that Mr. Carlisle had furnished the necessary for Doris Hatten's rent and Mrs. Carlisle knew it, pestering Skinny, and other items. I had been glad to testify that Skinny, whose name was Herbert Marvel and who ran a little agency in a mid-town one-room office, was one hundred proof and that, as soon as I had convinced him that his well-dressed male client was a female public enemy, he had been simply splendid. Of course, when Skinny had returned to the room after going to phone, he and I had had a full three minutes for a meeting of minds before the cops came. I had used twenty seconds of the three minutes satisfying my curiosity. In Mrs. Carlisle's right-hand coat pocket was a slip noose made of strong cord. So that was her idea when she had moved to get behind me. Someday, when the trial is over and Cramer has cooled off, I'll try getting it for a souvenir.

Cramer had refused the beer Wolfe had courteously offered. "What I chiefly came for," he went on, "was to let you know that I realize there's nothing I can do. I know damn well Cynthia Brown described her to Goodwin, and probably gave him her name too, and Goodwin told you. And you wanted to hog it. I

suppose you thought you could pry a fee out of some-
body. Both of you suppressed evidence."

He gestured. "Okay, I can't prove it. But I know it,
and I want you to know I know it. And I'm not going to
forget it."

Wolfe drank, wiped his lips, and put the glass down.
"The trouble is," he murmured, "that if you can't prove
you're right, and of course you can't, neither can I
prove you're wrong."

"Oh, yes, you can. But you haven't and you won't!"

"I would gladly try. How?"

Cramer leaned forward. "Like this. If she hadn't
been described to Goodwin, how did you pick her for
him to send that blackmail note to?"

Wolfe shrugged. "It was a calculation, as I told you.
I concluded that the murderer was among those who
remained until the body had been discovered. It was
worth testing. If there had been no phone call in response to Mr. Goodwin's note the calculation would
have been discredited, and I would—"

"Yeah, but why her?"

"There were only two women who remained. Obviously it couldn't have been Mrs. Orwin; with her physique she would be hard put to pass as a man. Besides,
she is a widow, and it was a sound presumption that
Doris Hatten had been killed by a jealous wife, who—"

"But why a woman? Why not a man?"

"Oh, that." Wolfe picked up the glass and drained it
with more deliberation than usual, wiped his lips with
extra care, and put the glass down. He was having a
swell time. "I told you in my dining room"—he pointed
a finger—"that something had occurred to me and I
wanted to consider it. Later I would have been glad to
tell you about it if you had not acted so irresponsibly
and spitefully in sealing up this office. That made me

doubt if you were capable of proceeding properly on any suggestion from me, so I decided to proceed myself. What had occurred to me was simply this: that Miss Brown had told Mr. Goodwin that she wouldn't have recognized 'him' if he hadn't had a hat on. She used the masculine pronoun, naturally, throughout that conversation, because it had been a man who had called at Doris Hatten's apartment that October day, and he was fixed in her mind as a man. But it was in my plant rooms that she had seen him that afternoon, and no man wore his hat up there. The men left their hats downstairs. Besides, I was there and saw them. But nearly all the women had hats on." Wolfe upturned a palm. "So it was a woman."

Cramer eyed him. "I don't believe it," he said flatly.

"You have a record of Mr. Goodwin's report of that conversation. Consult it."

"I still wouldn't believe it."

"There were other little items." Wolfe wiggled a finger. "For example: the strangler of Doris Hatten had a key to the door. But surely the provider, who had so carefully avoided revealment, would not have marched in at an unexpected hour to risk encountering strangers. And who so likely to have found an opportunity, or contrived one, to secure a duplicate key as the provider's jealous wife?"

"Talk all day. I still don't believe it."

Well, I thought to myself, observing Wolfe's smirk and for once completely approving of it, Cramer the office-sealer has his choice of believing it or not and what the hell.

As for me, I had no choice.

Printed in the United States
by Baker & Taylor Publisher Services